These **BLUE ASHES**
SELECTED POEMS 1982-1998

for Florence Maltese
en souvenir d'une rencontre
magique au bar Le Zénob
dans le cadre du Festival
International de Poésie de
Trois-Rivières.

En toute complicité
Jean-Paul Daoust

ESSENTIAL POETS SERIES 94

Guernica Editions Inc. acknowledges the support of
the Canada Council for the Arts.

Guernica Editions Inc. acknowledges the financial support of the Government of Canada
through the Book Publishing Industry Development Program (BPIDP).

The translator acknowledges the support of the Canada Council.

JEAN-PAUL DAOUST

BLUE ASHES
SELECTED POEMS 1982-1998

TRANSLATED BY DANIEL SLOATE

GUERNICA
TORONTO·BUFFALO·LANCASTER (U.K.)
1999

Poèmes de Babylone was published by Les Écrits des Forges in 1982. *Black Diva* was published as *Lèvres urbaines, No 5,* 1983. *Les garçon magiques* was published by Vlb éditeur in 1986. *Les cendres bleues* was published by Les Écrits des Forges in 1990. *111, Wooster Street* was published by Vlb éditeur in 1996.

Poems from Babylon, Solitude, and *The Magic Boys* were first published in a different version in *Black Diva: Selected Poems: 1982-1986).*

Typesetting by Selina, Toronto.
Printed in Canada.

Antonio D'Alfonso, editor
Guernica Editions Inc.
P.O. Box 117, Station P, Toronto (ON), Canada M5S 2S6
2250 Military Road, Tonawanda, N.Y., 14150-6000 U.S.A.
Gazelle, Falcon House, Queen Square, Lancaster LR1 1RN U.K.
Legal Deposit — 3th Quarter
National Library of Canada.
Library of Congress Catalog Card Number: 99-71657

Canadian Cataloguing in Publication Data
Daoust, Jean-Paul
Blue ashes : selected poems, 1982-1998
(Essential poets ; 94)
I. Sloate, Daniel. II. Title. III. Series.
PS8557.A591A272 1999 C841'.54 C99-900287-2
PQ3919.2.D25A6 1999

Contents

6

Eyes of the Desert

A blue valentine
Full of broken bottles
That the liver spews into filthy sinks
In welfare apartments
Scream my guts out
The shock of my tongue lolling like a necktie
The acid rock of the eardrum
Deflower my brain
Not laugh and pop the braces on my teeth
Prowl clad in pink in the dark
Puncture those desert eyes
The hair
Hysterical belts
The voice backing off
Hands that flatten out
Fingernails like dead fish eyes
Epic effort to lift the pinkie
Contemptuous flesh of life's corpse
Experiments on the heart's mirages
The weatherbeaten sign at the oasis
Sorry we're closed
Have fun with no coke
Can it be those lips that are touching
The moon is rubbing its black cheek against the sun
The surreal images in a sorrow's culture
The evening belongs only to Las Vagas
The window on the alley filthier than a neglected sore
These long nights with their deserted highways
In search of accidents

Tortures
Burns
Deserts have instant gestures of eternity
Just a lot of sand
Hard solid blond sand
Whips in the ultimate music of sandstorms
You'll die if you don't protect yourself
Silly passports
No one believes in them anymore
Desert fevers
Hysterical camels
Deep in hungry seas
The cinema's caravan
The air wrinkles with sere sounds
Fruit crumbles like snakeskin
New York snaps its skyscrapers like matches
The howling of cavernous skulls
The desert has wrinkles that terrify Hollywood
A footstep is only an ephemeral swim
A useless obstacle
A boring mirage
Here is where death preens himself
In full sunlight
The sand and its steel reflections
The eyes burnt to a crisp in fierce reflections
Well wouldn't you like a cold bottle of champagne
The desert like an overdose of madness
The eyes open their dams in vain
The silk of the nostrils can't withstand it
The throat is nothing but a furnace
The cancer of the moment
At noon in the desert there's a shower of suicides
Of petrified nightmares
Of broken loves
The heart
This lonely hunter and all

Dries up
Vitrifies
Come and see for yourself
Eyes of plaster
The desert has stopped weeping
The blood with its bald waters
Can't you hear the music of the ruins
Jeering amidst the vultures' feet
Or is it a hyena
These dates recalling certain halts
Nothing but a crust
When the sand shifts it's the better to kill
That final pose on death's horizon
The telephone doesn't ring in the desert
The rough palm that slaps
Claws in the eyes
Lenses that shatter
Already the blood dries
The desert of the morning of the evening
Sun or no
Here the seasons don't change
The mummified heart
Tenderness
A ring not worn anymore by day or night
The face nothing more than a rifled pyramid
Just another violated valley
The desert groans on the banks of the Nile
It's rough and tough
Las Vegas like a standing mirror
Finely chiselled
Pleasure's refrain
Brutal but effective mirror
A voice full of crevasse-deep wrinkles
The eyes of the desert move before they die
Like a TV screen full of snow
Here the absurd is only a passing invention

La Callas still sings on these sealess beaches
A howl that eats like acid
This sun
This desert

Egyptian Poem

I'll write a poem for you
In the Egyptian style
On your skin
Hieroglyphs of love
That our fingers will decipher
I'm going to mummify you
Wind you in wrappings
And kisses
Our careful ritual gestures
To keep you
In my eternity
I'll stretch you out
In the core of my heart
Where no one can go
Its beat is like music
To soothe you
To lull you
Love you
In the desert
Flooded with light
Our skin burning like sand
In the shade
The two of us
With our erections like obelisks of sacred light
Jealously guarded by the sphinx of love

1982

Solitude

Solitude. That blocks the eyes. Fatigue. And yet the desire. For passion. There where the *I* is most numerous. That stagnant state of the past. An *I* condemned. Another. Avalanche of black. Gestures of consolation are decapitated. Despair's hemorrhage. A strong poison to. Swallow. Last phase.

Solitude. That catapults toward nameless bodies. *A city is always full of them.* A pink cowboy. Who. Waits. With eyes like raw silk. That are paralyzed in mirages engulfing hysterical laughter. Make-up of the soul. But. We know that. *Face lifts don't work on the heart.* Solitude. Like a bitch you detest. But. That you tame. So she won't devour you. She takes us for one of her sick children.

Solitude. The *I* is bored. By. Your dinosaur smile. By beauty. When the *I* was WE. Is it illusion, just fabulating. Who knows. The diamond solitaire casts reflections of hate. Your full moon smile. Where the *I*. Lucky astronaut. Light. Eros in the Thanatos of the universe. And then. The fall. Into the void. The stars are plague carriers. And words that can't go on. And all that commits suicide at the bottom of the page.

Solitude. An *overdose* just by yourself. Too bad. In the body's computer, memory contemplates the gods of yore. On the aging screen of the skin appears an aging star. Like in a silent film. What raving. Fingernails get chewed like *popcorn.* While. The brain hallucinates. *Give me a break man. I'm dying.* But it all goes on anyway.

Solitude. Pacing up and down my neurons. Broken-down streets. An evening of acid rain. In the city. The skin makes a leap forward. And breaks. Wrinkles. The hair falls. Old age. Mirror of death. Solitude. Its spines. Cactus. In the opaque desert of life. *Everyone is afraid of a lonely writer.* What a *flop.*

Solitude. Each word kamikazes in its sentence. That no one holds on to. A feather undone from an angel's flight. Twirling in the hell of its fall. Like a *rock star.* Totally drugged. Washed up. Who's watching an old *hit parade* from the past. When she was at the top. But. As each sunset is peopled with jets flying in unison. That rise. But. *Crash at first sight.*

Solitude. Picking up garbage. Refuse-dump body. But of course. The brain looks like an intestine. And vice-versa. *Born for hell.* Live. On a credit card. Stolen. Full. *Blue millionaire.* Solitude. A bag-lady. Disfigured. By all those blows. Words vanish. Anemic.

Solitude. Climbing into the heart. A varicose vein ladder. A diabolical flood. *Purple rain.* Where the heart suffocates. The brain has blown up its dams. *Black out* for planet Body. The astral body. Extinguished. The ugly trees of March. Their turtle skin. In a nuclear sky. Where presidents travel. Popes. *Apocalypse time.* But. The bodies. Like rats. Making love in the sewers. Where the heart of slum city is rotting.

Solitude. But. The most beautiful love poems are written in a bed. That the skin remembers for a while. Look at that skin. Read what's written on it. Don't censure anything. Try. Read over again. Maybe. The beautiful moments it's lived. Tremble. When seeing. The passion of all those lips. That came there to drink. But. I'd be hijacked. Spied on. By paper James Bonds.

Solitude. Now. Alone. Like the tongue. A red carpet. Useless. But *I'm generous and I got style.* My fingernails in my mouth. Safety vaults. For caresses. Empty. Pillaged. Like tombs in the burning desert. *Wanna love before we die.* Should do it. But the dead. Alone. Who smell of death.

Solitude. It would take a miracle. To change this lyrical text. Into a luminous postcard. And this city. Crouched on the banks of the river. Like a crocodile. With fresh teeth. The *I* never thought it could go so far into. Solitude. Memories with their scent of orchids. The heart feeds its parasites well.

Solitude. Smearing the skin of my soul. Its cold kiss. Panic. Eyes. Modesty. Eyelids. That close. Curtains. Of skin. On an opera.

Solitary. Night. Distress. Of dawn. Arriving in its make-up. Make a drink. To fill. The grey hour. But. Solitude. As someone once said in a song. To the point of screaming. Lips open up like Marilyn's legs. In the flash of teeth all the world's sadness dances.

Solitude. Like a forgotten *cover girl*. Take your face in your hands. Because they are the last reservoir of caresses left. Fingers. Stems for faded flowers. Their worn out eyes. But. This void. Between the trembling fingers. Flags of. Solitude.

Solitude. Of the body. Moving forward. Like a parade float moving through a nameless crowd. Put make-up on my eyes. Black make-up. The better to show off my night. The sudden urge to laugh. At all that. The heart plunges into another glass. Alcohol. Sacred river wherein the heart purifies its pain. You cheer yourself up as best you can. Words. Ashes. On the beach. Grains of sand. In the Sahara of a life. Lips collapse on their porcelain rocks. Exhausted. Starving. *Nothing. Except. ME.* No one. And the body continues its voyage through the time of others. The sounds of conversations. *Cheap* operas. The *I* moves amidst its phantoms. The *I* clings to words. Final madness. The world is an unhappy place. Poetry freaks out.

Solitude. Of a winter. That's endless. Do the dead. The dead. Do they speak of the living. Of this new *mal de vivre*. That the dandies of this age parade before all. Decors change. Like the waves. Of a single sea. Suns of ebony. And. Limbo. Coma. And. Solitude. Blind. Deaf. Mute.

Solitude. Paralyzing the text. Photographed by a tourist *I*. Who will soon be knifed by the pain of words. *Life goes on. Not ME.* And the *I* goes into exile in a hotel of ice. Dreams don't grow anymore. Asphalted over. The indifference of others. Him. The eye harpoons him. In vain. *Moby Dick rides again.* And all the morons round about. *Jellyfishes.* A writer is fed up. Gets up. Goes and gets himself another drink. And leaves the machine. All alone.

Solitude. Like a panther. That's hunting. In the city. Where Tarzan is. Those skyscrapers. Phosphorescent baobabs. That the heart climbs. From up there it can fling itself. The city. *A jam session of lonely hearts.* Jets overhead. Mechanical insects. Taxis below. Roaring when called. Momentarily. But. Spiders spin in people's eyes the next *delerium tremens*. *Paradise is an invention of a mad genius*. Illusions. Physical though. Give up trying to make sense of it all. And. The ring. Alone. On the finger. Alone.

Solitude. That laughs. Fierce. Words. A caravan of them. The skin. In the sun. Storm. Over the cosmetic being. Carnage. Death casts his long shadow. Over the *suntan*. Solitude. Turning in circles. Like an electron. The pulverized smile. Slides over the eye's black screen. *Nobody. Loves. ME*. Enough material to write a text.

Solitude. Insatiable vampire. Each and every life gives its blood. And when the eyes turn inward they see nothing but madness. Alone. Like a Vestal Virgin. Guarding the temple of boredom. And there. No one prays.

Solitude. *No return*. No port of call. Just the mirages that the heart has consented to keep. Just a little game. Solitude plays games. Too. Loser takes all. Words. Jewels she gives herself. Luxury. She buys it. But at what a price. Every life pays into it. Always a loser.

Solitude. The *I*. Bang of a fist. On the concrete of cities. But her *buildings*. So much the star. Behind dark glasses. But there is nothing sadder than the end of a *star*. *Have you seen Bette Davis lately?*

Solitude. It's the cry of the stars. Styles. Who programs the computers. The verdigris of the screen. That can't imagine another thing. Other than the void. The brain explodes. In the absoluteness of its distress. *Tilt*.

Solitude. The cat. White. In my arms. Lamenting. Alone. What tormented spirit possesses her. Men have the eyes of volcanoes that children are sacrificed in. But. The *I* can't stand it anymore. Solitude is a light that shines on nothing but the void. And the blank space between these words. Solitary.

Solitude.

You feel so alone in the midst of words when the book is closed.

1985

Magic Boys

I have luminous nights. Where bold bodies shine. Their quick kisses. Startling nights. *And my life is a full moon affair. Like your smile.* My pharaoh eyes. But my hands are aging. On skins increasingly alert. My hands are limousines that are driving down DEAD ENDS. I have a Los Angeles face. Earthquakes. *More to come. Love me with all your skin, you dirty snake.* Beside you a rose is just an ordinary miracle. *And the leaves of autumn. The lips of death.* But tonight I'm miserable. *Ready to leave this planet.* These landscapes I know backwards and forwards where the suns set. My hands are drying out. Coral deprived of its seahorses. Where have you gone. *Help me. Someone please help me. It's a rock'n'roll prayer. But there's no God.* I need an angel with perfumed fur. His feathers fallen down my neck. Love you. Love you. Love you. Fingers don't move fast enough as they try to feel that ephemeral dazzle when your skin drives me crazy. I'm screaming because you kissed me and that was what I wanted. Till I'm drunk from it. Till I die from it.

Everything has an end — even death, do you understand?

EVERYTHING HAS AN END — EVEN DEATH.

Now let's talk. The better to see the mirror that reflects startling images back to us. *How amazing. But I don't know you. And you?* Your powerful eyes. The Vatican shies away. Moscow gives up. The Pentagon forgets. *When you're powerful. It beats God.*

But I'll let your skin tell me other tales.

His cattleya eyes. When he puckers his festive lips. His teeth are full mirrors. Has to do with porcelaine too. Who boldly dared frame his bold body. Every gesture like a sheaf of light. Fingers have smiles that lovers alone detect. Has to do with soaring. A skin is a fascinating land. When lips sculpture the heart. *It's a smile. For Eternity.* Eyelashes have plumes. You like a sun in my eyes. Your Jamaica body. The surging. Into time. Our lives. His candour when he turns toward me. Who's watching him. His eyes are two wings of bronze. His terrace smile. Where I leisurely drink my pink champagne. The heart at last rends its shell. Free as Tarzan among the vines *sniffing* an orchid. Question. The petals answer. *He loves me he loves me not he loves me.* Our resourceful bodies. Dancing. *All night.*

He's making love right this minute. I know. With someone else. What can I do about it. Except stare at this motionless fog where the evening is vanishing. His silence. This burning moment that's consuming me. Don't panic. WHATEVER YOU DO. Otherwise disaster time. Wait. For it to be over. For him to come back to me. For him to want me. Plant my teeth in his neck to scare his blood. Clutch his hair. My claws unsheathed. Another swan is dying. May apocalyptic fury be celebrated on our tongues. I walk delicately through the apartment. I explode at the least squabble. I'm an atomic bomb. Crazy crippled telephone there. Old thing. Deaf. Dumb. If he were here obviously everything would be just fine. Obviously. I'd be bitchy to him though. Like *an extra large all dressed* pizza with a double order of anchovies *a Chinese dinner for three* five St-Hubert BBQ chickens obscene telephone calls a telegram singing: *Fuck you. Fuck you. Fuck you. Fuck you. Fuck you. Fuck you. Fuck you. Fuck you.* But my body is eating the silence. Barely moving except to grab a rum and coke. And put it down like a piece of ebony. Very chic I don't even wipe away a tear that starts down my face. Lava. A new wrinkle. Because of him. The TV is on. I can hear it buzzing. America and its mechanical presence. I'm so anxious for him to come home so we can both laugh. At us. The hesitation before the first kiss. More tears will follow. The heart is in eruption. His transparent dross. He really is making love to someone else. Maybe he's in love with him. Maybe not. And when he comes back he'll have that champagne smile of his. He'll bury his lying eyes in my skin. But he'll come back. Until then all I can do is wait. Everybody's lived through what I'm going through. So what's the matter except my pain. More poems are stuck in my throat. It's not that I'm afraid of comparisons. *I know who I am.* But him. So far away suddenly. Perilous sirens sing in my tears. Sad eruptions from the eyes. The WE is foundering. Night. A punctured eye. But there's no big deal. He's just making love with another guy. My words are submerged in tears. Angels with damp wings can't fly. Alone. My heart as it writes screeches like fingernails on a blackboard. The picture is empty. Eyes blaze in the storm. And the day is rising. Its crooked smile. And those immaculate sheets. Like a shroud around a death-stricken heart. Mummified.

☆

It's snowing. Words. The page. Passive.
I've always loved you.
My skin. Deserted beach. Where I grow sand roses.
Castles as bright as your eyes.
I've always loved you.
Your hands. Made for picking the rarest of flowers.
Your fingers folding. On my lips your greedy tongue
        gathers words.
I've always loved you.
It's snowing. Suns. You're beautiful. Like a Viking on his
        drakkar.
En route for his conquest.
I've always loved you.
In your Himalaya arms. I'm playing. The yeti.
Don't you remember.

I'm Ramses II.
I'm building crystal pyramids for you.
I'm your magician.
I've always loved you.
Like the spring loves the swallows in the sky.
I've always loved you.
My angel with heart of jade.

Novels are needed to depict all that. Poems to stigmatize those loves. Other trophy texts for the trembling flesh. I wear my skin like a new alphabet to be deciphered. Us. Accomplices at last.

Oh yes, we are magic boys.

These words in your ears attentive at last to our becoming. Our excitement. Our lives on vacation. For ever. I'm dreaming. Wide awake. But I dare to give in to the drive to want to be happy. Whereas all around me is fascism. Its rotten codes. Tortures. So love me more. This text where I survive as though in a hothouse. I'm afraid. The medieval fortress. Haunted. Its dungeons. I'm being pushed into the battle when I'm trying to work in my alchemist's lab.

I'm a sorcerer. My powers will make the magic boys arrive. At last.

I don't want to be burnt again.

Now is the time when extraordinary guys discuss their becoming.

Their caresses. Their starred fingers.
Their tragic skin. Daring to hope.
Now is the time of the magic boys.

1986

The Sleeping Angel

I'm watching him as he sleeps. His skin, relaxed. Beautiful angel. His eyes sheltered. In their enchanted settings. I'm watching him as he sleeps. His skin lying there. Trustingly. I put out a finger. And move it about. Over his eyelids. Their silk. I feel his eyes smiling. Calmly. I write words with my fingertip. Tender words. That I don't dare say to him. I'm frightened when he's afraid. Sweat. My desire like misty rain. I'm restraining myself. So I don't pounce on him. Like a tiger. But. I retract my nails. So I can stroke his sleeping body. His nice soft fur, so soft. Feathers. I'm watching him as he sleeps. I shiver. What if he decides to leave. Or get out of bed. Or spread his wings. And fly away. My heart stops. Stops dead. Total despair. Black. Cold. My finger stops writing. I'd like him to catch these words with his lips. I'm hesitating. Should I go on. Only he knows. Me. I want him. He knows that. I'm watching him as he sleeps. In the pearl-grey morning. Lying on the bed. In all his glory. A blue-blooded angel. While he's asleep. Is he pretending? I'm weaving a net around him. Around us. My finger is now in his curls. Amber curls. But what I'm really staring at is his lips. Incredibly beautiful lips. Delicate. But strong. Serious. Maddening. That's where he's hiding. I'm venturing into his lair. With my fingertips. Just the tips. Velvet tips. I know he's worried. But I'm doing it anyway. No one has ventured there before me. I know that. But I want him to know that I'm an angel. Just like him. And that I love him. His lips are opening. Is it for a kiss. Or to bite. No reason for him to be defensive. There's no one attacking him. My lips are close to his. Ready to take them. To touch them. To rock them. I didn't know he was so miserable. So fragile. And so decided at the same time. I'm waiting. For him to move. He's opening his eyes. I'm caught. In the act. Like a thief. Of images. He's looking at me. He doesn't condemn me but. Maybe a reproach. I'm not moving. I'm terrified. Like a child on the brink of a lie. He puts out his hand and it frightens me to death. But he places his hand on my shoulder. As though to console me. He wants me to go to sleep. But does he realize what state I'm in. How insane I am. And suddenly I'm the one who's snared in his arms. I struggle. But I have a feeling he's going to win. I remove my fingers from his hair. The way you remove an orchid from the jungle. But I loved playing the parasite. I imagine the two of us in the sea. In the waves. In the sunlight. The salt I lick off his skin. As the blue of the sky veers and falls like a gigantic curtain so we can see the stars dancing. The moon. The universal goddess. And him. More lavish than all the lavish spectacles in the world. True. I'm sleeping. With him. And I'm dreaming. What about him? I want him to speak to me. To take me with him to his country. I've glimpsed incredible landscapes. Insane. There are exotic gardens in his eyes. In his eyes where it's always summer. And his body's performances absolutely stun me. Solitude crumbles away to dust. An expired idol. He has changed my outlook on life. Put a stop to time. That sleeps with him. I hold back my tears. My cries. My desire crazed and wild. But. One movement and he catches hold of me. The shock of affection. Again. In his lips I'd sign any and all pacts. And I'd give my soul to the devil with a laugh on my lips. *How can I sell something that I don't have anymore.* I'd change myself into a fierce dragon and shield his body from any attacker. *Love isn't a joke.* When I move my lips up and down his body it makes incredible music. Music of the angels, you might say. He can hear it too. I pile up postcards on his back. Fragile gifts. I can't get enough of his kisses. Caress after caress after caress. The wild country he takes me to. Where he has never dared take anyone else before. I feel like a barbarian. I'm looking at him. I can see he's surprised at having come so far. Like being in a new land. Both of us amazed to see that it really does exist. Worried too. Nervous as two angels flying in a magnificent but unknown sky. With unhappiness lying in ashes somewhere else. In forgotten places. His California face. Where I'm a traveller. As blissfully happy as a movie star. His arms are as sophisticated as the Ritz. With its panelled rooms. Its sparkling afternoons. Its farniente. At times his gestures are unexpected. And surprise even him. When he moves closer to kiss me. When his jeans explode before my eyes. The heart clings. To his skin. And falls off with a song. Sublime diva in a made-to-measure opera. Every passion unleashed. Irresistably modern. I'm watching him as he sleeps. My amazement at his being there. So close. His pores are breathing. Like flowers. My fingers are restless. And write love letters to every part of his body. To tell him things you're not supposed to say. Too bad. I can't help dropping messages all over his skin. Little multi-coloured parachutes. Invasion. His eyes roll in their sockets like certain sunsets. Under closed eyelids. On mornings of cool light. How to make him happy. How to destroy his defences. So I can talk to him about happiness. About our being together. Just the two of us. In a bed where our members are in love with each other. Members of the same sex. *So what.* I'm watching him as he sleeps. Like a guy. In love. He's sleeping. One arm is folded over his head. As though buried in a sheaf of nervous plumes. Waging war is out of the question here. Or being the other guy's nazi. Or his shark. My lips continue their promenade along his skin. On his neck. And they sow blazing suns there. To chase away his shadows. His cold nights. Write him what he's afraid to hear. But what he knows. I don't want to be cast among the nameless. Their petty limbo. I want to take him to a hundred Tahiti lives. Let newer New Yorks be built. And cathedrals. Their flamboyant crystals. I want him to love me. I want him to fall into my arms. Nervous. Excited. And I want him to give himself to me. AT LAST. I want him to shed his skin. And leave the old husk to scavenger birds. My finger touches his new skin. Proud. And his whole body turns its petals toward love. I have images in my hands. That I gather from his skin's offering. Yes I'm watching him as he sleeps. And all the images I've gathered I spread out before me. And gaze intently at them. Before making a sumptuous bouquet that I'll hand to him when he wakes up. And the more I harvest the more his hardy skin yields. He is an incredibly rich angel. I succumb to the madness. Of this angel ready for anything. I'm watching him as he sleeps. Like a sailing ship riding at anchor. Peaceful. Not a single wrinkle on the surface of the air. Music. Tam-tam. The heart proclaims the glad tidings. *Me and him. The angels of love.* So close. He's sleeping. And my fingers are dreaming. He's a beach that no one has seen. I discover its fine sand. Almond. His eyes. Two mahogany suns. I soar into the sky as I once did in the gulf of Siam. But that skyscape was empty. Now the sky has a face. And the heart is a dazed astronaut. The impetuous beauty of that universe. Yes, I mean yours. Where I'm floating. Free. Happy. And I want to show you other flights. I know your body. Intelligent. Your clever hands. Your violent desire. So come here and we'll take off. I stretch out my fingers. Gazelles in the savanna of your hair. You. You're sleeping. Fabulous beast. And I feel so good. Protected. My fingers are dancing on your skin. And you're amused to see me acting so crazy. You make fun of me a little. To conceal how you feel. You look around you. But there's no one there. No one. Except US. So you take a risk. Your fingers dance with my fingers. And your skin and mine stage a ballet with very moving choreography. You grow tender. And you spread your big body like a fan with disturbing designs. I'm watching him as he sleeps. The angel with the bountiful body. I withdraw my fingers. Except for one. That glides over his forehead. Comes back to his eyes. Your eyelid trembles. Slightly. Then calms down. And I see that your eyes agree. In harmony. With our desire. For EACH OTHER. And my finger continues its glide along your nose. A little fall and it's on your lips. Soft carpet. But with passion for weave. My finger catches. On your breathing. Your body murmurs. But doesn't move. My finger continues downward. Along the chin. The neck. And I can't hold back anymore. My lips curl around your skin. And I start to purr. Happiest of cats. I'm listening to you as you sleep. I'm stalking your dreams. I close my eyes. Like yours are. And I can see you. You were expecting me. And we soar. Into the blue of the air. Two angels. AT LAST. Happy.

1986

To Be Happy

To be happy
I can say
That I've applied make-up
To the void
Put more teeth in smiles
Than the smiles could contain
In the heart
Enough energy to blow up NASA
And all the alcohol in my veins
Just an immense pain
To solitude
To loves that have collapsed
Ah the domestic disasters
My poor life
To the beat of *what's going on*
I've wandered from mouth to mouth
I've kissed teeth true and false
I did everything to be happy
I was supposed to do
But in vain
The formula has not yet been found
At every real wound
The heart bursts
Like an audience
The aorta pops
Because the heart is on a stage
That collapses
To be happy
I could tell you things
That'd send shivers through you
Because
But there goes the heart
Ensconced in a fake galaxy

The police catch up to me
And kill me
Because to be happy
You always do things
That make you tremble all over

1986

BLUE ASHES

Blue Ashes

A man of wounds
From knowing sex so young
Six and a half years old
From knowing death too early
My thoughts turn when wood burns
In my restless mouth
To when other children were learning
To spell I was counting the names
Of my lovers especially one
Baptized with the sin of the flesh
Not yet at the age of reason
I was a child violated
In the loveliest of landscapes
A forgotten-prince sandbox
Where king cobras coiled round my thighs
The combat of different doctrines
Yet I liked to watch his penis pleased
To see me
Even though I had no notion of love
Certain bodies should be silent
When a child molested in a woodshed
Finds his surroundings so unfeeling
And hands so vulgar
My penis so young
In the fireplace flames are nameless angels
Lovers writing their doomed poems
Like all children I was curious
But there was one of my lovers
With eyes of harp

He looked like the angel behind the altar
In the church of Notre Dame de Bellerive
The one who chases others out of Eden
A frenzied rhythm rushes through my blood
Stories that are not to be told
But quick hands consume many a desire
My body welcomed many a pirate
Now that I am alone with my age
The remembrance of those stories haunts me
Desires rooted in vertigo
I should have killed him earlier on
But what does a child of six and a half know
The fire inside me is limpid tonight
Despite my Niagaras of flame
The arcs of your eyes in a sky imagined pure
Tonight I'm a wolf-child howling
At our restless bodies our caresses
They have grown insane roots
For my written life to write
As if I could be saved from madness
That special feature of intelligence
My body still holds fresh your touch
When I was six and a half
And I had a lover
Where is he now that I have him
I want my text to quiver
I still oscillate in the light of his desire
Was he a faun
Who was he
Other than his desire
Memory and its fatigue
I need him still
I think I do
My first love
Words can try to fit
Rings on hackneyed fingers

But to no avail
Except for two fingers
Undoing his fly
And the other fingers helping
What kind of child was I
And what kind of man was he
Hair all over his body
An ebony fleece
A mature man
I know that now
But then I was
Already excommunicated
Before my First Communion
Yet I regret nothing
Except my ignorance
Everything seemed so normal
In the splendor of May
That lethal bay where the boats
Are water lilies but
Sly tricks don't help
Bodies lashed by autumn's passions
When words fall and scatter
I was a child drugged on the penis
Especially on his
Not understanding a thing
But a willing participant
Curious about our curious happiness
He was always there
When I wanted him
But who was he
With his hot brand am I
Like him now
Vampirized by his desire
What year is it when
I touch his penis again
Time falters but not I

My hand is direct
Words pound at me
The other children didn't like him
Called him nasty names
Were some of them my rivals
With my parents or friends
I never wanted to say
His name
I wanted only to feel his big hands
Tender on my miniature body
Slowly but surely time
Chases all away
Classify my memories of him before
It's already too late
They smother us sooner or later
Can we live over what we lived once
It was always at dusk
When the sky was awash in the blood of suns
And the undersides of porches turned into
Labyrinths
In the chiaroscuro of ordinary evenings
When he would tell me I was late
With his eyes wide open like his legs
He asked me to love him
I was six and a half years old
I was insanely curious
I was the navel of the universe
The wind was singing as with one hand
He was busy splitting wood
And with the other he
Would undress me
Until my hands were completely
Swallowed up in his
I had just entered the lair of the dragon
A neighbor at her incredulous window
Let go of the curtain

Like a token of her helplessness
The old-fashioned autumn cast golden sequins
A landscape of tropical skin
In what century are we
His arms were huge
Like those of giants
In cartoons
But I wasn't too fragile
More nimble than a squirrel
Just amazed at his big body bent
Over mine
A great love story
With the lake as impassive witness
I was a child sacrificed
In the arms of a loving Moloch
I knew what to be lovesick was
Before I read stories in school
In his arms I found the only life
I was God in the land of his madness
Yes I loved him
I loved him
Even at six and a half I needed him
To live
Years on years
The body's presence has vanished
How to call up memories
When the brain has lost the scaffolding
Of remembrance
That seems to always get the upper hand
Was it under a September sky
When he pulled me closer
To his body
Was it under a Venetian sky when he abducted me
From a stupid stretch of lawn
I loved him
He did too

I was six and a half years old
And him
Strong and superb the way I wanted to become
Entering the hallowed woodshed
Spreading his legs wide apart over logs to split
Colossus of Rhodes
I was the faithful sailor
I was only six and a half but
I knew what I was doing
I know he loved to love me
Tonight fatigue and alcohol
Words would like to fall into place
And be done with it
Once and for all
Yet I can see him
A love story
His pain
My body growing up would've surprised him
Maybe even been too much for him
Maybe he'd have turned in some moments
Of our ecstasy
He was so strong so solid
His hair too long too curly too black
The child of six and a half giving in to his demands
Since life seems to require it
When he comes toward me
An erotic poem
He spreads his legs opens his arms
He speaks to me
As I reply
Sunsets never before seen engraved on the sky
And other useless miracles
Yet our movements are sublime
Become ours and no one else's
The wind blows now over our skin
Through the cracks of the shed door

I can see him splitting wood
Now I watch him feel him touch him
Tease him
Like the wind flirts with the water on the lake
And flips it back as it blows
Our names he says are engraved on the waves
I open the door as it grates on its hinges
He stops at once comes up to me
He picks me up laughs presses me to his broad chest
Throws me in the air and I laugh
I turn into a shooting star on his sweaty torso
He holds me by my feet
My face buried in his jeans
He laughs and I pretend to be scared
A cat diving into the air
The different angles our caresses make
In the blue light of evening
In the church the incense wafts upward and away
The trembling light of the tapers
I loved him
Like the sunset
He was part of
Programmed in spite of ourselves
To love each other
He didn't know how to defend himself
Against me
Doomed to sit between his arms I'd listen
To the river as it sang
Operas so melodramatic
And yet I was afraid of him
Of his demands
No talking to anyone
About us
Be like the frozen lake
Melt into the mishaps of legendary tales
But there I was back again in his fur

The fire burning quick with warmth
The ritual chopped wood omnipresent
Dry memories crackling
Our bodies blazed in secret
Without mentioning telling verifying
What we wanted to be
Your thighs
My little hands would get lost in them
You had a touch I remember
Radioactive
No one knew anything about us
No one wanted to know anything
Who can understand this story
Of bodies caught in the cogs of desire
First and forbidden
Under his long black curly hair
His blue eyes
I never imagined eyes could catch fire
Like his
Burning as they say
With blue flames
When the sky is ablaze
Because the sun goes away
When he asked me to love him
Because he was the most unhappy person
In the whole world because he was
The most beautiful
The water nearby whispered old love poems
That I learned later on
The ones not taught to children
When his penis drew closer to me
The tree of good and evil
The winter wood to be chopped
I stared at him
Amazed admiring
My lover loved me

I learned what love is
While the other children of my age
Were learning to recite their lessons
I was learning how to inflict pain
At the alphabet age
Caterpillars butterflies ants
Grasshoppers give me juice or you're dead
I made him suffer when I'd not show up
When I told him never again
When I'd run away for no reason
Fear
Of him of myself of others
I'd run to the lake
Screaming my terror
My rage
At him
Sentenced to silence he watched me run off
His big hands in tears splitting the wood
But not as precisely as I chopped his heart
A love story
But I was only six and a half
He was in his twenties
I'll never forget his body
Whenever I saw him
His body's smell in the shed
The sweaty wood
That I never found elsewhere
In the sterile air of the elementary school
The nuns like wax statues
At times the stale air in the confessional
Would hint at his perfume
His shoulders broad as church portals
Where I loved to be
The ritual of our caresses
Always in a chiaroscuro setting
The paintings of Caravaggio

That I understood the minute I saw them
Except it all took place between the rue Tully
and the boulevard du Havre
In Valleyfield
Where the bay is the stage
For the most beautiful sunsets in the world
Clouds in a frenzy behind the belfries
Of Notre Dame de Bellerive Church
Tipped over tables said the priest
But the water of the lake
Blessed by Satan
Where I would plunge after lovemaking
How could I purify myself
At six and a half
How could I purify myself in those waters
Gothic cathedral mirror
Condemned excommunicated
I was preparing for my First Communion
My heart full of you
But my soul was very light
It's a love story just a love story
So banal
How to make it believable I loved him but
There is nothing to tell
You try to understand you know afterwards
It doesn't change much of anything
Six and a half years
Time to be happy
He loved me
He wasn't a relative
A young neighbor in his twenties
Tall and strong and beautiful and tender and passionate
His hair was black and curly and long
His eyes blue like lakes mirroring the sky
A smile like a ship all lights ablaze
Shoulders where I could sit and ride

A torso thighs a penis
A body that still excites me
When I was a child Reason awakened
Deep in the heart
He gave me what others
Would try to take from me
He was only twenty
And a few years more
I was six and a half
He loved me
I loved him
I loved burrowing my face in his chest
I could hide all of me there
No one could ever find me
Sheltered from every stupid thing
It was always noon with him
We were in love for years
But I grew up
And he didn't change
I left him
In the fire
Calling him names
The way we do to those we think
Are hurting us
He loved me
And I loved him
Does he still love me
In his bouquet of ashes
I will always love him
Despite the call of other bodies
Water always flows away from us
To elsewheres of love
But his big body leaning over mine
Hallucinated by my memories
His weeping willow hair
The body struggling

The heart delirious
Magic memories
It was a love story
Made of passion quarrels renewals
He liked to check through my report card
I was first in my class
He would reward me
A love to kill any comparisons
He often wept in my little arms
At times I was sure his axe
Would be used on me
Our quarrels
He was twenty
I was six and a half
He was my hero
We read Tintin together
He explained the pictures to me
In Nepal in Bokhara I thought of him
Who had shown me the beauty
Of the streets in that village
Where I had already strolled at six and a half
With my lover
Long black curly hair
Blue eyes
Together we laughed at the antics of Martin Le Malin
He gave me books
I read a lot thanks to him
I took a stroll on the moon with him
With Jules Verne and him
Always him
He made me carve our two names
On logs he had cut
Engraved in fire
A jackknife with an onyx handle
A gift from him
From you after your return at last from Mexico

So we could both laugh
At the boy scouts
His eyes were blue like a mournful Sunday
Or like the bay when it takes on
A festive air
Before the regattas came to spoil everything
The logs for our hieroglyphs
That way you said we will burn with love
At times I'd scream awful names at him
I thought he was dirty
I avoided him
I didn't want my schoolmates to see him
To get to know him
Jealous
At six and a half I was possessive
Whenever my mother and her friends would say
Why doesn't such a pleasant young man
Get married
I'd shut myself up in a closet
Insane with rage
But he's married to me
Who can understand
At six and a half
Melodrama is part of all passion
I'd rush to find his soft lips again
So blue in the reflection of his eyes
My hands sheltered in the hairs of his chest
His heart beating wildly
Drumbeats of the Iroquois
I'd start to cry
We'd turn to Tintin again
He was the Yeti
But promised he'd not harm me again
I couldn't say no held tight in his gaze
Feelings are so violent
At six and a half

I was a barbarian in the silk of his hands
That held back from caressing me too much
I know there were days when I entered
The schoolroom
Lustrous shining
More so than a newly polished brass bed
Because he knew how to love me
And I too learned
Two lips two rhymes
Does he still love me
The waters of the bay are still there
The belfries the satin music
It was always at sunset
In the doorway of the woodshed
Orchid shapes of light never the same
As though the angels huddled there to watch
Our ritual unfolding
He shouted his admiration at my growing body
He was more beautiful than the angel moping
In my little missal
I said my prayers to him
I loved him
And he loved me
He was risking his life
I didn't realize
How could I understand at six and a half
He asked me for nothing
Except my love
I had a feeling death was prowling nearby
When we love we are afraid
We will lose the person who is our life
How can I relate my desire for him
Every day
My father told my mother that
I was having nightmares
Playing hop-scotch hide-and-seek

In the sand of the playground
Or tag
The others were afraid of the bogey man
But we were making love at the time
When the sky convulsed
In a final kiss
We had to part
And pretend
To go to sleep
The parents were waiting
While he was afraid of smothering me
Daring to give me one last hug
And yet I had fingers like claws
And we would always carve
On our wooden logs
Our initials
While his eyes would be like swallows
That think they are attacked
Sometimes I'd go there
In a pout
And he'd carve the logs by himself
I was reproach incarnate
With my little hands on my hips I'd challenge him
Dare him to touch me
From the height of my six and a half years
I defeated him
Another David but
On days like that the wood chips would zoom
Past my head
Shooting stars or meteorites or bitter words
I didn't give an inch
While he brought down the wrath of heaven upon us
So deep a gulf between us all of a sudden
But he loved me
I loved him
Our blind bodies would always find each other

Everything started over again
Twilight evenings when we said nothing
Imagining the winter to come
Weeks sometimes without seeing him
He said he would go insane
The other children disliked him
They didn't trust him
But I loved him
Yet I never defended him
When I made up my mind to go and see him
He'd be waiting in the woodshed
Cutting wood for winter
I'd appear from behind a snow bank
In my toque and with my red nose dripping
Which he could lick
He'd throw himself on me like a wild man
And warm me up
And push me down among the cords of wood
And make love until we were dizzy
And then he'd bury me in logs
He raised his axe
The holy pictures of the Old Testament
Abraham and Isaac
Whack
And a log was split in two
That's what I'd get if
When he bellowed I was leaving him I'd laugh
And finally he would too
We were so frightened
All of that was so real in the Bible
He loved me
I loved him
Skaters on the frozen waters of the bay
My brother some friends
But I was in love
At six and a half you can do anything

He was the great tyrant with blue eyes like
Snow
My guardian angel
I'll always be six and a half with him
The air around him was so warm
He loved to stretch out his arms and pick me up
With one hand
While the other
Drew me close to his lips
So he could lick my neck
I'd scream
He would tickle me
That'll teach you
Then he'd lick me all over
A cat
I watched his penis rising
I was only six and a half
Him so old
He knew a lot of things
How to relate them
With the precise forbidden lighting
Of those moments
Denounced from the pulpit
While a Sister of Providence
Screamed her dictation to the class
I never made any mistakes
He made me carve words in wood
That I learned from him
Words of love
Like the hymns to the Virgin Mary
Him and his skin sweet as mauve lilacs
Outside the churches
The splendor of his body
The sins of the flesh
Those soft summer evenings
His name scrawled on the school walls

Why me
How a child of six and a half can love
I remember
How big his fingers were
Strong and tender that laughed at mine
We read Tintin in the light streaming in
Through the cracks between the boards
His smile still makes me shut my eyes
Blue as the bay
He loved to kiss me
While my mother was on the porch calling me
Where were you this time
Mommy it's me it's your little boy
The light lets out a roar when the sun leaves
He could cast glances
Impossible
Eyes like those sunsets
When Venice collapses exhausted by light
Now I know the metaphors
Does he remember me
And my eyes he drank deep
My small hand in his hand
That traveled
He explained to me
Tintin on the Moon
With him my interest in traveling began
With him my interest in living began
While death was watching us
Behind the door
It set ablaze
When he loved me too much
And it was time it all ended
But the poem flowed along
The waters from the lake into the river
Where Russian ships they said would sail
Offshore those islands

Where monsters lurked in the lee
Stories not for children's ears
Whereas he told me everything
I learned about blame from others
My voice beating time with his blood
He loved me
I loved him
A love story
I was only six and a half
He was in his twenties
Beautiful a statue in a church
I was an angel in the creche
The one who nods his head at each offering
He loved me like no one else
Ever afterward would love me
Now that the winter nights are long
More indecent more adult
How I would have been loved
I learned to run fast so I could jump into his arms
Wide open as the bay
Gentle as its waters
Appearances transparencies
Mirrors of demons
Yet angels flew about us
Silence from the priest
Useless asking me for his name
Intertwined with mine on the bark
Of the logs burning our imperial crests
He really did love me as he often said
Lies alibis for the parents
We made love in the setting sun
That made the lake bloom with light
And the water into scarlet poppy fields
Even the perch as they swam admired
The anarchy of the sky
The flayed colors

I loved him as we love only once
The magic of our first love
What's the use of other love stories
His honey blue eyes
His eyes always took on the color of things
Even in the evening
Blue diamonds
His man-of-blue skin
Eyes that sing for children
In deserts teeming with mirages
In my father's rowboat he'd spirit me away
Captain of the grandest shipwreck he'd say
Against his skin of flannel wool I'd huddle
Sheltered from all the stupid things of life
While at church I was travestied into little Jesus
Dressed in my pink robe I blessed the whole cathedral
From the pulpit of my childhood I watched the bishop
Watching me
While I pronounced the sermon the priest had written
In my carefully learned diction
On Holy Family Sunday
When the creche was closed
When little pink Jesus returned to limbo
When I walked the grandiloquent aisles of the cathedral
In my silver satin slippers
My heart was still full of you
Who had just made love to me
Who made me arrive late for the ceremony
With a triumphant look I said to all
I had met an angel
I had just left your arms
Always so sweet
Angel hair taffy
You bought for me at the circus
Such a charming neighbor said my mother
I was furious with you

Didn't want ever to see you again
For days and days
I had seen you cheating
With my mother
But you loved me
I loved you
The way a child of six and a half
Can love
The other children didn't like you
Were afraid of you
Gave you nicknames
I didn't care
They couldn't know
How proud I was to carve in secret
With the jackknife you had given me
Our two names in a heart on the bark
In the flesh of the wood
Initials
Etched in blood
The family kneeling to say the rosary
My little dog Sunny shivering nearby
Watch out
Stop or you'll go straight to hell
The cardinal droning mysteries on the radio
While I was discovering yours
As you brought them to my mouth
I loved you
You loved me
The way it only happens once
You cut logs
To give warmth to your family in winter
While I gave warmth to your body
I traveled through your fabled land
While you read Tintin to me
As he traveled through the Amazon
My heart was broken

On the moon
Where you promised we'd go one day
Stories stories to be written down
Our names still burning in the fire
Of those sunsets that remind me
Of you and me
Sweating under the sere trees
Of autumn
Don't disturb children
Reading Tintin
On their knees of passion
As they learn to read life
And to write it down
Even if death can come of it
I know
That I killed you
On a cold evening in May
When I accepted to grow up
And grow old
You were found
Your head in the wood stove
Burnt to ashes
He had a seizure
People said
A dreadful accident
People wrote
He caught fire
While our carved logs were burning
In unison
I loved him
You loved me
But the sun sets as before no more
I know now the color of blood
So alone
You and your arms of a giant
It's true I was only six and a half

And sneaky
But I learned things bigger than life
We were heroes
In the blue warmth
Of summer evenings
Of winter evenings
While swimmers were in the lake
While skaters were on the lake
We were in love with each other
His skin of blue mink
His eyes where a thousand suns exploded
Threats of the bogey man
That made me giggle
The giant who read Tintin to me
While others were deciphering holy pictures
Buying little Chinese children for a quarter
He would stuff me with chips coke black licorice and red
That he despised
Because they left a curious stain curious smell
On my lips
That he would wipe clean
With the back of a big hand
Where I'd nibble at the soft hairs of midnight blue
And I see from other texts
Other films
That you were the marvel of my world
I loved to make sketches of him
And then show them to him
That he collected
And kept under his mattress
When I watch the sun playing
With the afternoon waves
I can feel metal butterflies in my throat
Mist in my eyes
I see his strong body again
His eyes and their color from far-off lands

Waiting for me
In the doorway of the woodshed
His lips opening like a dazzling tear
Across the white of his teeth
There he is
Leaning against the doorframe
He says nothing
He looks at me
He waits for me
To come near
I duck under his arms
The door slams behind us
Door to a vault
Say nothing to anyone
His refrain
He was afraid of me
He despised me
He wanted me to vanish
They found him his head burned to ashes
His heart at rest at last
Such a good-looking man why
And me behind the tales
With my secret
Window
Rain
Watching time pass
The time that saw us
Because he loved me
And I loved him
I was only six and a half
He was twenty
How can anyone love more than that
At six and a half
Reading now about great stories
In great books
I love him even more

When I'd bring back my fishing trophies
Perch sunfish sometimes bass
His voice close to my ear
That tickled
He took me away for a few hours
Or was it a few seconds
He took me to his land of love
His eyes almond-shaped
In them the sky copied poses
The poses of the light
In the blue droplets of your sweat
When you loved me to the limit
Of your strong body
A big lake
Warm and blue
While through the cracks in the planks floated
The dust of angels dancing in the light
As you used to say
The dead leaves the wind hurled at us
I'm still afraid of their rustling
But your touch aroused the dying light
Our story was a story of setting suns
You wanted me to grasp each shade and hue
To be tomorrow's relics
There are bodies that stamp
Their surprises their wonderments
Are indelible
Like yours
Stripping the ornaments of a Christmas tree
Because to love is to go openly to one's doom
Your teeth of blue ice
I decided to love him
The way one decides to say to a grasshopper
Give me some juice or else
Here is a love story
Unacceptable unforgettable

Useless epithets but indispensable
The ornaments of love
He died his head burned to ashes
His heart crushed
Between my crab claws
That crush today's day
In the castle of yesterdays
Where the centuries still watch
The madmen who concentrate
On the pain in every passion
In the arthritis of my fingers I think
Of your warmth
When we carved our names
Scars intact
That the fire propelled heavenwards
My heart mortgaged for life
In the luxuriance of his arms I forgot
The harsh lessons of growing up
The blue refrains of his skin
I'll never be able to sing of them enough
The blue forbidden to the angels
The only color they cannot reach
Now make room for the legend of his eyes
When the blue veers to the grey of Paris
His caress will never have troubled
The discrepancies of shared nights
The grand hotels
Where it is only words that quiver
But his I Love You
Along with his smiles
Often upon the water
The blue of his eyes suddenly appears
Humiliating me
Staring at me
Before his body's leap toward me
The opera of his back

His Olympian penis
And all that touches upon memory
That's where I learned to read
To write
To live
I liked to see him in torture
Ready for death
When I wouldn't show up
When I played the nonchalant David
When he hesitated between reproaches threats
And a caress
That always won out
We played cowboy
He was the bad guy
I had to kill
Bang bang you're dead
He'd say watch
And would rise again
The snow falling outdoors
More blue than a poem
White words on the page mirror of a lake
Frozen as the moon
That recedes
My eyes now short-sighted
Where so many horizons mingle
The storms where all things seem to die
The page turns white again
Because it's winter because
Words are exhausted in their quest for order
Because fear's been keeping his eye on me
Since childhood
When I suddenly became a grown-up
In your arms
Where I was king
Who understood nothing of his kingdom
I loved to breathe in the smell of your hand

When you'd put it on top of mine
And write on my skin a manuscript in Braille
That you could read so well
I can still hear your stories
And yes and I repeat you did have blue skin
Your eyes made rustling sounds in the foliage
Of your eyelashes so black so thick
You and I
Was it so terrible
Six and a half and you
Twenty
In the blue sand of the snow
Your words drifting snow past my ear
Carved into my very blood
Tonight a writer is leaning
Over the hallucinatory well of his childhood
Falling like Alice and it's you again
Who picks me up
Who tells me to calm down
Especially not a word to anyone
I swear I'll never tell
I'm scared scared
All the way from the height of my six and a half years
I'm falling
Into the blue brazier of your arms
Fear of falling
In love
Your deep purple muscles
By a miracle I'm writing in our perspiration
Sweating shrouds
Condemned to eternal torment
The Sisters of Providence always say so
The parish priest says so
Like those children of Islam who are tattooed
With passages from the Koran
On their backs

Or on their solar plexus
Your fingers are hurting me
Stop stop
You let out a bellow lift your axe
Stormy weather again
Foam on the waves of your lips
The advancing snow roaring
You hug me in your arms
As though to smother me
Then you put me down
Open my picture book
Paste angels in it
Pink and green and blue
You scatter them
All over my body
And paste them with your tongue
All over me
From head to toe
Like a filled up scribbler
I'm crying
Because I can't stand it anymore
You the barbarian
Too impatient
At the end of the rue Tully there's the bay
A dead end
To the right there was an old shed
That's where I learned
What eyes choked with desire
Could suffer
In the waters of the bay I imagined
Fish of gold mermaids of green
Enchantments spells
Because of you
I have seen the Mediterranean
From you
I understood the pain in every glance

Your hand around my neck
So tiny in your octopus hand
Tentacles surrounding me
That's when I decided to kill you
You bent towards me and said
Don't be afraid we're safe here
In "this pitiful shed"
I can hear you clearly now
In the empty luxury of hotel rooms
I hate you
For the fake gentleness of your words
A story book wolf
Because of you I was never a child
Like the others
You stole my childhood
But what do I know about all that
But I did cry more than they
Already jaded by caresses
Solitudes like circles
Around my sleepless eyes
You said you liked to watch the light in my room
Go out
I was a faithful lover
From one caress to the next I didn't understand
A thing
Your eyes were beacons
Now in the tumultuous trek through other encounters
I always have the taste of death in my mouth
In the flickering snow of our cinema
Where I can watch a porno video
Your penis bigger than my arm at the time
You would say but look at yourself
You're growing up
I loved him
You loved me
I was only six and a half

You were twenty
People will despise you for that
Not me
No one after you will have that blue
In your arms in private I always announced
No vacancy didn't I
In the bay the sunfish still swim
Their backs like old strips of tires
Sometimes you licked my skin raw
I'd start crying
You said you were sorry you got carried away
I forgot everything in the color of your eyes
While my mother was humming
"I listen to CKVL twenty-four hours a day"
You were polishing my fingernails with your lips
Mirrors wherein Narcissus would gladly have died
Are you happy where you are now
Do you still ask for the same things
Do the seasons still exist
Do you live
Here only words exist
To force you to come back
Where gods roam
In blue landscapes
Singing and playing the saxophone
Your eyes were felt-tipped pens
Your words clear blue
Palimpsests of love poems
Long ago all that
You who risked everything for me
Our shouts cutting through the light
Sharper than the axe through the air
We loved each other as in a marble palace
In a Taj Mahal setting
You'd say it was the last time
Your tears of blue

I have never seen the same color since
I'd shake you by the shoulders
Like those landscapes of snow trapped
In heavy crystal balls
Your eyes snowed blue
I love the snow because of you
You and your white tiger eyes
But you were so young
And I so old
Now that I know everything about love
Your initiation
Into the delirium of the unsaid
Let the words rain down
You loved me
I loved you
But I was only six and a half
In the scandalous embrace of our bodies
You whispered songs to me
Tunes that were popular
Colette Bonheur Edith Piaf Lucienne Boyer
You dropped them into my ear
You kept a watchful eye on my haircuts
You were old at twenty years
But me
Did you give any thought to me
Who was only six and a half
I want to punch you again
As you hug me tight against
Your hot body
I'm struggling and you're shouting
I'd like to pitch you into the fire
The way you throw those logs
Witnesses of our lovemaking
Sometimes I would tease you
To make surrender more fun
You learn fast when you're in love

It's a known fact a child
Learns fast
If you could have seen his eyes
I've grafted them on to mine
And made them into a flag for the mind
Into standards unfurled for eternity
Because it's blue
In the rumpled disorder of beds
But we never made love in a bed
It was in a castle of wood and sheet-metal
Facing the loveliest landscape in the world
Facing sunsets organized
By lovesick angels
I still love him
Wherever he is
From the height of my six and a half years
I was thinking of him when the nun told me
You're not paying attention
You're trying to get attention
When he was unshaven his beard hurt me
His adult male skin scraped my skin
I'd had enough of his rough-and-tumble love play
The blue fire
So violent in his eyes
In his lips
In the thick veins of his arms
Like hot mauve serpents
At times when he'd take off all my clothes
From head to toe as he said
Or when I go and see him
When I'm sure to find him barenaked
Behind the wooden door
That grates on its hinges
I see him huge strong and
Pitiful
I'm confronting the god of love

Theseus and the Minotaur
In the purplish blue of the air
I swear impossible oaths
Poetic sonorities
I still love him
In the restless gold of sunsets
Over Venice Bangkok Beirut San Francisco Rio de Janeiro
I think of him
His head turned to ashes
That I'd have liked to throw into the bay
Sometimes I'd go running into the shed
Kamikaze
A technical question
Of surprise encounters
Make him come and leave him
With his remorse
I'd go and join the others
Playing cowboy
Through the spaces between the wallboards
He would watch me helplessly
He wanted to kill me
Bang bang you're dead
My fine Indian brave
Because I had just told him
I give you five minutes
Then I'm gone
Just time enough to smoke your cigarette
The axe twirled in the sultry air of summer
The winter will be a long one
His arms like slimy eels
His eyes like startled fish
Imprinted with weary waves
The prism of his eyes
Water with mauve fires
He was reduced to begging me
At a time when the electric chair was in use

What is left of our love you would sing
You molded me
This very minute I use your words as I speak
In that haven those rays of light
Where the stained glass of Chartres would drift
Sometimes your eyes melted
Like snowbanks
Like old people when they decide
To die
That sky forced to bear witness
No such thing as an expert in love
All of its chimeras I met with you
My mother on the porch calling me home
You had to let me leave then
I knew what I was doing
I left his big body more fabulous
Than the river so near
Than the Nile so far
But I have to stop now
The person I love is reading this text
But I still have your fire at my fingertips
To be snuffed out
Made into full moons
Made of frozen fire you told me
I was only six and a half
I believed you
The way I believed in guardian angels
I always left mine at the door
So he could keep watch
With yours
Before going to see a Walt Disney film
Your eyes were seared blind
Because they dared to look at me
Now I am twice your age
Your eyes were too blue
Or was the snow too white

Or the alcohol of today too pure
Is blue the color of childhood
And pink the underside
To soften the cold
You had arms like elm boughs
Where I loved to climb
They have vanished
Like you
My grandmother sitting on the oak swing
You went crazy
Don't tell anyone not a word to anyone
It's our secret
You bent down to whisper another one
In my ear
I love you
I walked through the big grassy yard
As through a sleazy back alley
With make-up on my heart
I was leaving my beautiful blue-eyed lover
But I was only six and a half
He was in his twenties
A question of lacerations
The snow of his teeth
Dazzling enough to frighten children
But you're growing up you'd say
But I could never catch up to you
In catechism class we were told
Of how the Virgin appeared at Fatima
To the three young shepherds
I was a well-behaved child
But it was you who appeared to me
Always ready for love
Your body's erotic din overpowering
At times I hated those sturdy arms
That plucked me from my world
Spirited me away from everything I knew

I was afraid
Of him
With him
Frightened to the bone
But some evenings
Shaped the sunlight into lyrical landscapes
When the blue incense of the Carmelites on rue Santoire
Swirled and vanished into the chapel's vaulted ceiling
Me in your arms
You who were pillaging your life so you could love
My life
My body as white as a sheet
You tried to get to speak
By tickling me caressing me
That's enough I've got to go
It was time for the whole family to say the rosary
When I could pass in review our caresses of the day
And how I'd managed to braid blue gold tresses
In the fur on your chest
At the same moment in that ramshackle shed
The spiders were spinning the web of our fates
Where our lives were caught
Ready to be devoured by time
An offering in the mouth of an unknown god
There were times neither one of us spoke
Tacit mysteries
Get-togethers frightening in their passion
There was always a gale in your hands
Your nails smelled of wood
I was a body that learned to germinate
In the hothouse of your embrace
The blue windowpanes of your face
Because of you my body later on would be
Of brass and my eyes of eighteen carat gold
My heart of solid silver
Desires made of platinum

Incomprehensible dreams
The habit of a certain form of tenderness
Especially that first one
You haunt me
Vampire you fascinate me
With your Egyptian eyes
Eye shadow of my insomnia
Find him again in the maze of words
Despite a hideous death
He committed suicide it was whispered
Not too loud the kid might hear you
Understand
Such a charming young man
Another insane mishap writ on the waters of the bay
On the blue pages of a lake another crazy story
Flows into the river
As only small towns can tell them
When the body has told all
It goes on repeating over and over
Insatiable old men
I recognize them now
Those bodies brushed
By butterflies with new-blown colors
Beyond the memories of sunken loves
Their stubborn doggedness
The child who didn't want to die has killed
The blue lover
Killed the Minotaur
I used to lick his face
With a tongue of fire
His face rendered unrecognizable
By the blue waters
Fed by my desire
Staple food of all passion
In the Golden Triangle certain orchids
Brought to mind the spectacular display of his eyes

Their blinding failure
Eyes that have left their mark
On mine
Their sumptuous markings
He was my Surprise Arrival
The great god on my path
Whenever we met by chance
In the warm waters of the bay
I would swim away mute as a fish
Between his legs floating
In the collusion of the waves
We'd play
Two dolphins
In his eyes danced adventure films
Where I was the star
Zorro Tarzan The Lone Ranger
He plied me with candies
For the films projected on Sunday afternoons
In the basement of Notre Dame de Bellerive Church
It was the only time my parents could make love
I thought of him
His face on the screen
We were the heroes
The blue perfume of my first love
Concentrated in the deepest folds of my memory
Why at six and a half
Was I plunged into that hell of love
Nights when I would howl your name
In the morning I'd lie to my father
Already my Fellini look
I wanted only to rush to see him
Until then I'd scratch our names
In the sand of the playground
In the chimerical waters of the bay
In the vaporous air of morning
On the windowpanes

And then go to him in secret
Make him groan with pleasure
Especially me knowing I did
While for the tiny grey lives of others
Ant-like displays are being organized
How then can anyone not envy us
My blue lover and I
My beautiful love burnt to ashes
Horror film
Sometimes on a street corner I'm afraid
You'll suddenly appear
To take revenge
On me
Say your real name
To fool you
Say it out loud
As a child I had to bury it
In the sand of other games
I was unfaithful to you
They said you threw yourself into the fire
A half-wit they said
But did you really die
In the shed
Bang bang you're dead
You had only one way of rising from the dead
At the autopsy I always had to perform
But I couldn't do it that time
But I never believed you were dead
No one could recognize your face
But I could have
But how could anyone suspect me
Of hitting him over the head
With one of our logs
Of pushing him headfirst into the stove
Of running away
Of going home as usual

A detective poem
Whose ending I'll not reveal
I pretended
To understand nothing at all
Not to be affected
The nights I screamed from the loss
Of your touch of your smell
Of loving you as much as I hated you
Your hugs your threats
My brain is tired
A death flickers on every mirror's blue screen
Cover them as in the old days
With plain black cloths
Behind them you still watch me
But I was only six and a half
To each his own memories
They buried you
Alive in my memory
The sun can't serve as excuse any more
But who burned that day
If it wasn't the two of us
Like our logs carved
With all our secrets
Corpus Christi Sunday
You led the procession
Proud radiant like your torch
Followed by the pastoral groups
The Daughters of Isabella
The Ladies of Saint Anne
The Lacordaires
The Knights of Columbus
The schools
The men's group
The women's group a bit behind
The religious congregations
The priest's voice over the loudspeaker

While swallows skimmed over the waves
The trembling flames
En route towards a repository
Laden with sweet-smelling flowers
You so beautiful so proud
You winked at me
While I was standing beside the priest
Disguised as an altar boy
Watching you with pride
Better for me if you had never existed
When I look out the window
And follow the tracks of enigmas
In the hours on the misty panes
My blue lover
I've searched for you in so many windows
You who were always alone
Waiting for me
I was your destiny
Everything seems so simple now
I was in communion with you
With all my being
It made me ill
I cried with shame
You held me in your arms
And rocked me
He would tell me
Soot is raining down on your heart
Someone had to pay
I killed him
I had no choice
At six and a half you don't understand
You know
How to sort through all the blue ones
Keep the good one
Throw the others
Into the fire

With a light heart that's what I did
Like electrocution
But if I activate my memory of you
The above fiction makes me uneasy
Blue as well
The image blurs
Into a bad photograph
The setting suns take over
Postcards of trips
You famous in my child's heart
Of six and a half
You wanted it thus
Life pushed to the death
A classic of its kind
But your well-endowed thighs
Forests of the Amazon
Your penis
Anaconda
Now
In my contemporary dreams
You haunt me
Polar stars
I use to find my bearings
As when I skated on the frozen bay
I'd look up at the starry sky
Looking for
What never came
The forbidden fruit in the woodshed
Seasoned with our tears
That we bit into
Your arms an altar
Where I was immolated
Is there a hell for children
Who liked to sin
Who learned words
They knew they shouldn't know

Words of love words of hate
Of lust of lies
The others didn't count anymore
I loved you
The way you wanted
Me to love you
But I was only in the first grade
At the Bellerive elementary school
Sister Lucille was so nice
She'd offer me her little Chinese children
For twenty-five cents
I was a missionary too
Out to baptize all of China
Or a White Father in Africa
In the Philippines
Our shadows
Cast by our dim caresses
In that woodshed
Where you split wood
Summer and winter
Where we never tired of carving our names
The names of love you said
But what did I know
One doesn't know everything at six and a half
Now this text
That you will never read
Just as well
Love is a mishap more often than not
Yes I did drink in the blue waters of your eyes
Stronger than the purest of alcohols
Too perilous
At times in the evening alone
In the lighted pool
The feeling I'm swimming in your skin
As I once did
I'm frightened

Panic in the lighting
Night is terrible in those pools
Unbearable the swollen blue
All our primal fears
Dinosaurs evil genies
Like you
More evil than the most evil
Yet I loved you
I kept a dream secret from you
To become Professor Tournesol
And invent some device
That would reduce you to ashes
Burn you at the stake
Like a sorcerer in the Middle Ages
But I was so little
In the falling snow
In the winds of autumn
In the perfume of your arms
The refrains from those days transport me
But when I caught you
With another
A young neighbor boy
I swore you would die
Yes I did see the two of you
No I wasn't spying as you said
I thought the two of us were sacred
You told me that
Who burned whom
My revenge will be terrible
The gestures I thought unique
I ran away
Screaming
Towards the spear of the Gothic cathedral
Reflected in the deep purple bay
Of Valleyfield
I had sacrificed everything

For you
My father my mother my brother
My boyfriends my girlfriends the parish priest
The bishop
Sister Lucille
The neighbors
Everything and everyone I tell you
A log thrown at your unfaithful head
And pow
Your head in the flames
My silence like lead
I still loved you
Cold sweat down my back
So soft you used to say
I hated you
Enough to kill you
Everything is mixed up in my head
Fear joy disgust
You're there even at *tantum ergo*
Between notes words
Our caresses
In the deserted streets
The cold brings back to me the void
That is you
The headaches
Afterwards
My feverish eyes
Eyes like little lanterns you used to say
But afterwards
Inflammatory rheumatism
My heart mortgaged for life
Hate you hate you try to forget
To live
Our love my love
What do I know about what really happened
About living at six and a half

He was found with his head in the stove
Burnt to ashes
And the smell
The woman next door terrified
Her heart on fire
I was reading the Old Testament
Delila in Samson's punctured eyes
Nebuchadnezzar and the Maccabees
Sodom and Gomorrah Abraham and
You burn forever in hell
Yes Father
His hair all burnt off
What a smell
Implacable blue outside the window
I'm only six and a half
I go to the elementary school
I'm first in my class
I'm a model pupil
I tell them I often go down to the basement
Where there is a door to the outside
I tell them I go there to do my work
I always tell the truth
He is being buried
In the clamorous light of May
The lilacs mauve because so blue
Like my headaches
The sudden fear
In our caresses
What year am I in
He's taking me with him to the end of the world
On one of the steamers sailing past all lights ablaze
Russian ships or Norwegian ships
Where the sailors are impossibly blond
The spice route
India China
Your body

Where I lose my way take a wrong turn
The Baie des Chaleurs
You're shouting between my two hands
And I get angry
And you want to hit me
And you kiss me
You ask my forgiveness
Never never never
I'm only six and a half
I'm vomiting
Because you make me sick
But in the stove inside my brain
Your hard head catches fire
I hate you
But you love me isn't that so
So beautiful so blue clad in your twenty years
But I've never read a story like ours
Words
White as your teeth
Like the snow falling
Bold insolent
Time parallel to tales of love
How can I trust you
Who killed whom
Who burned whom
My blue lover
But I was only six and a half
One is fiercely jealous at that age
Run away into the following idea
Kill him
He's like a nasty Walt Disney hero
A nasty Tintin
But I've never been caressed
The way you did
You were a better teacher
Than Sister Lucille

Your body was a marvelous blackboard
Where I loved to write the alphabet
Of our trysts
Destiny puts its trust in children
But you are drifting away from me
As the moon from the earth
The stone from the fruit
For the glacial blue
Right in the palms of your hands I wrote
Our destinies
But you said
Children believe in nothing
Except spankings
Caresses candies
I found there was nothing else
Your Venice eyes
Your violet penis
Your abundant fur
Evenings when strong winds blew
We could groan as loud as we liked
When the waters of the bay
Were whipped into waves
Then your tongue would fill me
My ears overflowing
What dimensions caught us up
We were not ourselves
In the thrall of what magic spell
In the labyrinth of my bones
You are still alive
Despite your ashes
A statue of clearest marble
Your eyes of a beggar
On my streets
And the bay like a song
Where you would wash your strong body
In full sight of all the children

Watching you in silence
Insane with admiration
When the soapsuds sparkled
You dived into the water
Like a burst of laughter
In our throats
You didn't have the right
To make me jealous like that
Near the grey pebbles of the beach
You resurfaced ten meters away
With a great splash of wind and wave
Your hair today Buenos Aires
At moments like those I'd run away
Yes you will pay dearly for your show
I want to see you on your knees
In penance
Your tongue can go all around
But not touch me
The great ruins heaped on the horizons
Where the green is swallowed up
Six and a half
Already too many memories
Of love
The others the additions
Your eyes of forbidden blue
Your jungle laughter
Your airport poses
That I recognize as Polaroids
Unthinkable our multiplications
At six and a half you proved
One can love
Like you
At twenty
Strange Romeos
To give you the shivers
The splendor of a body that wants you

Serious
Grave
He drank me in with his two big hands
Filled with tears
In those oases
Every mirage was possible
Now the lilacs have turned into dates
The waters of the bay indelible
But I know each movement of his hands
Maybe
Was a cry
His stormy eyes
That polluted me
In the homeliest of settings
Yet we had fun
Like the reflections of the two churches
In the bay in Valleyfield
Experts in love
Who was the sorcerer who attended my birth
Who sold me to him
But he was barely twenty years old
I was six and a half
We were in love with each other
I killed him
Such a handsome young man people said
My mother her friends the neighbors
He had a body like a sin to confess
No absolution possible
But the whispering water in league with the sun
Your Gauguin skin
Desiccated cinema
My skin soft and smooth
Polished pumice
A child's skin
Of six and a half
My eyes of the desert frighten you

Your hands on my chanting Indians
Dying for revenge
You're the bad guy
Bang bang you're dead
The victory totem
Now standing in our laughter's museum
So radiantly blue it blinds the fires in our eyes
That are in love
In spite of me
In spite of both of us
Ashes among the stars

III WOOSTER STREET

Wooster Street

For Lise Lambert

It's raining on Wooster Street
Where I live like a painting by Edward Hopper
Where I listen to the song of the city
As it floats through the clouds
Where the buildings drift
Like lanterns lit by angels
From my window on the fourth floor
Of 111 Wooster Street
I can see the pigeons bathing
In the honey from a street lamp
Where a man is stacking garbage
That might be scattered later
By party guys with little to do
Like the other night
And from my window vantage point
I watch the artists at work
Painters photographers dancers musicians
And who knows maybe another poet
Listening like me to the words of the rain
Falling on Wooster Street
Where I'm in my immense white loft
With daffodils all over the room
As yellow as the taxis driving past
On glistening Wooster Street
Where spring rains softly down
Not like at home in Quebec
It's raining on Wooster Street

The Singer

For Madeleine Monette and Billy Leggio

In the bric-a-brac din of the New York subway
A blind woman's burned-out voice is singing
An old blues that cuts your heart in two
As neatly as the formidable white cane
She uses to get her bearings
As she gropes her way around the car
Her other hand holds a cardboard cup
Where a muscled colossus drops a green bill
Thank you she says
As she continues her walkabout
That bothers lots of passengers
As her voice hacks out crazy words of love
In the stale air of the subway
Where wary eyes watch her every move
Sometimes her worn throat emits a crystal note
Surprising and puts wonder into life
Like the two lovers leaning
Their beautiful faces closer to each other
And from respect have closed their eyes
The better to get inside the sad song
Of the blind black woman walking along
Like a modern Oedipus
In the subway of Megalopolis U.S.A.

A Stroll

For Martha Townsend and Matt Darriau

Sometimes you see in the sidewalk cement
High-heeled shoes etched in pastel hues
Accompanied by the following words
Beauty covers New York
Near Washington Square
Under an unflappable sky
Outside the Citibank door
A black is panhandling
A dime please just a dime
Above the subway tunnels
Where people take shelter
And huddle in tribes
The city vibrates and like a dragon
Belches geysers of smoke
While long and silent limousines cruise
Like efficient sharks
One street leads me to another
To displays of luxury's compact excesses
I go into a Soho shop
A splendid saleswoman holds up a blue jacket
Made of raffia and linen
In the City I play my part
A dandy happy to be lost at last
In the center of a mosaic of faces
Constantly shifting constantly rearranging
Demented choreography where I say to myself
I'm suffering but it's too beautiful for words
And across New York as it dreams wide awake
The night is spreading its diamond lacquer

Enjoy!

For Maurice Tourigny

Through the amber veins of the streets
I'm strolling along very Proustian
Finally a tourist of myself
Night suits American cities
The bigger-than-life anthology of their bodies
The restaurants the bars
Where wall to wall angels wait
Words on fire in the evening's ink jostle and jump
Shhh! Enjoy! whispers the spring breeze
Streaked with dark flashes where the young and beautiful
Parade like bold bits of blue from heaven
Shhh! Enjoy!
From beyond the evening's grave this ritual
Love trail on Lavender Lane
Booming from the loud speaker of my heart this voice
Shhh! Enjoy!
On the luminous canvas of New York
The full moon seems so small
Alfred de Musset would probably rewrite it
A dot on a gigantic I
Out of an open door like a cat
A jazz tune slinks its way
The sax notes fall in golden rain
On a beggar slumped on his bench
With a hood on his head
Looking like a lost monk
Beside him a man noosed in his tie
Is reading Zen Comics
Over his head crucified on a tree
A poster for heroin addicts
Call us when you're ready to get off your high horse

But in my ears the wind keeps repeating its mantra
Shhh! Enjoy!

Dean and Deluca

For Nelly Benmola

At the Dean and Deluca café on Prince Street
Convoluted arabesques of conversation
Abstract paintings always trying to trap
Something concrete but different from what's said
Words wilt like flowers
In the troubled waters of many an eye
And left on the beach of language
Like goldfish
Asphyxiated epithets
But all of a sudden in a chocolate-coated silence
Two lovers hug and kiss

Downtown

For Dorothy Berryman

Alone in his room like a big bed
He's thinking at the window
As New York softly taps
With its wings of congealed gold
So he gets up gets dressed and walks toward
Washington Square where skinheads hone their knives
On the fountain's cement
All around are vendors of hot dogs and pretzels
Nearby is New York University
Where the doomed poets of Greenwich Village are studied
The yellow taxis always surprise him
They look like toys besieging the streets
Of Manhattan where it feels good to walk
As in a poem

Memorial

For Keith Primi

In the middle of the night
On an East Village sidewalk
A painful memory
A canvas in honor of a dear departed
A black and white photo in its gold frame
Of a handsome smiling young man
Lying on its bed of purple velvet
Lit by the flicker of a candle
Where a few red roses wither and fade
Above the title of Thomas Mann's novel
Death in Venice
From that little glass mortuary
A sudden glacial draft escapes
Coiling around my feet
So they can no longer move
And powerless I stand there
On an East Village sidewalk
Gazing upon the touching details
Of this epitaph plunged
Like a knife
Into the cold night
Where the specter of AIDS
Is grimacing

Last Curtain

For Shibata

It's raining in the subway
Grey rain
Like pillars and rats
My weary eyes close
In a mechanical movement
Where the lids collapse
Into their worn curtains
Exhausted they open again
Upon an empty stage
Where Gregorian water falls
In a sinister basilica
Where I realize my old body
Is the only possession I own

A New York Prayer

For Yolande Villemaire

God I need money
Lots of money
My health's OK
Thanks God
Got my friend too
Thanks heaps God
You've always given me
Everything I asked for
But now I want to thank you
A million million times
For the millions you'll be giving me
Which for you is nothing at all
But it's really important to me God
Because you've got to believe me
I really need money
So I can forget I need money
And besides money I've got everything I need
Oh send me money God
Lots of it
Oh my God please
Oh you've no idea how grateful I'll be
I'll go up the steps of the Shrine on my knees
Like Imelda Marcos in Saint Patrick's cathedral
You gave her what she wanted
So now it's my turn
To have money
Lots of money
Quebec culture will be better for it
I swear it God
Hurry and send me money
Lots of money

Like you did for Rockefeller
And for a lot of others
For every thousand dollars received I'll light a votive candle
I know you like votive candles God
And I'll light them just for you
To thank you for sending me lots of money
Lots and lots
I need lots and lots
It's not a luxury
I just want to live every day like an orchid
So send me God some money
It's just paper after all
It has to be green though
We agree on that right?
American green
You can exchange it anywhere
Very handy
Oh you're cool God
I know you're going to say OK
And give me lots of money
Lots and lots
The votive candles are ready
I'll light them all over the map
From New York to Paris
Tokyo to Venice
Rio de Janeiro to Shanghai
Montreal to Mexico
And wherever else you want God
Name it I'll be there
I'll take the Concorde
It'll be faster to light them that way
Oh send me lots of money God
Lots and lots
I'm not trying to buy you God
I just don't want to turn atheist
Let's say a million for starters OK

That would really help me out
And we'll see later on
Think about it God
A poor poet offering you all those candles
All across the world
Wouldn't that be a celebration
So it's settled then God
Oh thank you
Oh thank you so much
You won't be sorry God
Ever ever
I'm not asking for the whole golden calf
Just one slice
A nice big twenty-two-carat slice
Of rosy gold
Oh I know you understand me God
I want to be even crazier
I want to live life to the full
I don't want to have to work anymore
Oh give me lots of money God
Lots and lots
Make me part of the filthy rich
So I can regain the earthly paradise
It has to happen God
I need it to happen
Like oxygen for my lungs
Like love for my heart
Like sex for my body
I need money
Lots and lots of money
And I'll give some away
I'm generous by nature you know
I'll buy drinks for everyone
Pay for trips for all my friends
I plan to start up a press for poetry
I plan to change the face of Quebec literature

I plan to give it a face lift worthy of Elizabeth Taylor's
Oh answer me God and send me lots of money right away
Lots and lots
You can't say no
With no material problems
I'll really be able to live like an angel
Live like I want and spend like I want
I'll be able to make peace with my bank manager
Don't be cheap God
I know you can be at times
After all you're supposed to be
The patron of this damned planet
Where you can be pretty tough I know
Anyhow
You know the pleasure there is in giving
So be infinitely kind God
Infinitely good
Infinitely powerful
And send me money
Lots of money
You're so rich
And it's said we're created in your image
So it's time you did a few touch-ups on us
And sent me some money
Lots and lots of money
I don't dare ask Satan
Don't trust him
You're the one who should give me some money
I'm not asking you to be just
I'm just asking you to be generous
Remember there's lots of filthy rich people
Who don't deserve to be
But I do
So make me a millionaire it's my turn
And think of all those nice candles burning
Like the lights on Broadway

Where I'll write a sequel to *Jesus Christ Superstar*
Oh send me lots of money
Lots and lots of money
And I'll donate some to the nuns
Like my mother always did
Don't wait for me to be old God
Do it now
It's urgent
Time is money you know
But of course you know everything
So c'mon tell me where I can get some money
Lots of money
So we're agreed
I'm not going to sell my soul to you
It's yours for the taking
Likewise my body
Or what's left of it
Oh God hear me
A million bucks or two would be so nice
Interesting
Intelligent
So my God it's up to you to give
Money
Lots of money
It's all I want
Because I've got everything else
I promise I won't be a snob
Just contented
So it's a deal
Oh am I ever going to thank you
Down on my knees
With votive candles all around me
Oh thank you God
But God it's important this be clear between us
Don't come for me like a thief in the night
Come for me only

Only
When I've spent every last penny

Fourth of July

For Julie F. Pareles

He's standing in the gay bar on Christopher Street
With more than one rum and coke under his belt
After all it's the Fourth of July
He's wearing a shirt with the American flag on it
Pre-washed jeans
And cowboy boots
Of course
Then he leaves the bar to ogle
The Empire State Building all festooned
With red and white and blue lights
That follow him as he walks
Towards the East Side to see
Fireworks courtesy of Macy's
The biggest department store on earth
Of course
But when the multicolored rockets
Blaze into the Manhattan sky
And explode in a dazzle of din and colors
Amidst the shouts and clapping of the crowds
He too roars with joy
In the shadow of the skyscrapers
As they share in the grandiose spectacle
Slipping smoothly over the mirror's glass
Of the East River nearby

Washington Square

For Esther Charron

In Washington Square
A sprawling young man stares at another
And with his sunny razor blade smile
Skillfully pares away his black jeans
So his muscled legs leap into view
Near the fountain where the blacks are rapping
Bodies tumble everywhere in the light
Like so many ferocious petals
A policeman roller skates slowly by
An old black man clowns around two girls
Smile girls smile why don't you smile girls
And I'm the one who smiles
But I notice two lovers
Reading in the grass
His head rests just below her breasts
His hairy chest is naked his legs akimbo
He's holding at arm's length The Castle by Kafka
Between the book and his chest's lawn
His lips float in a pharaoh-like smile
With one hand she balances a book of Walt Whitman's poems
And the other strokes his shoulders' tattoos
Where a hefty dragon is spitting fire
All over his rippling muscles
When she shuts her book and leans down
To kiss him
My heart isn't in it my body either so I take off
To try and forget the disquieting scene
Repeated over and again
All over Washington Square

Rendez-vous

For Pascale Gousseland

New York is knocking at my window
With all its teeth a-dazzle
And tells me get up
You had your beauty sleep
Now show it!
A honey of a wind sweeps across the graffiti
Where I'm sauntering along
Like a passenger ship come back
To salute the great green lady
Lifting her golden torch
In a rambunctious toast
And I leave Soho for Christopher Street
Where many a karma is knotted and undone
And I just love it
My heart pulses in muted beats
My eyes sparkle like polished brass
With make-up meant to please the pharaoh I am
My arms move like efficient wings
Tonight is the night
And if I'm smiling it's because I know
The Poem won't miss the rendez-vous

BOOM

For Lena

BOOM
SOHO
SPRING STREET
TWO O'CLOCK IN THE MORNING
OF COURSE
I ARRIVE
WITH SHANGHAI
A SHI-TZU
A BLACK AND WHITE TIBETAN MONSTER
A LINE-UP AT THE DOOR
BUT THE BOUNCER
BUILT LIKE A GYM
GIVES US A SMILE
HAPPY TO SEE US
AND THE GOLD ROPE LIFTS
LIKE A VELVET DRAWBRIDGE
AND WE ENTER THE BAR
FULL TO THE RAFTERS
OF COURSE
IT'S ONLY NEW YORK YOU KNOW
LENA THE CUTE ITALIAN BARMAID SPOTS US
PRESTO A GLASS OF CHAMPAGNE SPARKLES
ON THE MAHOGANY BAR
FOR SHANGHAI
OF COURSE
MY RUM AND COKE COMES NEXT
WITH A CROWN OF LIME SLICES
AND IN THE OVERCROWDED BAR
THE CRAZY MUSIC BEATS UP A STORM
AROUND THE PRETTY GIRLS
AND OH BOY THE PRETTY BOYS

WHO PAT SHANGHAI
LUCKY HIM
AND I STARE AT THEM
I GIVE MY EYES A TREAT AS THEY SAY
IN SOME CORNY OLD POEM OR OTHER
AND WHEN I FINALLY MANAGE TO REACH THE BAR
AND PUT DOWN SHANGHAI SO HE CAN SIP
HIS FRENCH CHAMPAGNE AND ME MY CUBA LIBRE
MY EYES TAKE IN THE LOVELY LIVE SHOW
GOING ON RIGHT NEXT TO ME
REALLY SO CLOSE
OH WHAT LUXURY SUFFERING LIKE THIS IS
AND WHILE OTHERS ARE WAITING OUTSIDE
SHANGHAI LAPS AT HIS CHAMPAGNE
DECADENCE ALWAYS HAS A STYLE OF ITS OWN
EVEN MORE SO AT NIGHT AT BOOM'S
OF COURSE
AND THE EVENING DRUGGED ON THE WHOLE CITY
MAKES EVERYTHING LEVITATE
ALL THE ORGANIZED SOLITUDES
WHIRLING AROUND ME
AND ALL THOSE LIVES SO BEAUTIFUL TO SEE
BUT SHANGHAI JUST CURLED UP IN MY ARMS
THE TIME HAS PASSED SO DELICIOUSLY
IT'S LAST CALL ALREADY
THEN I TAKE OFF AND SAY TO HER
A MILLION THANKS AND SEE YOU TOMORROW
BABE
AND I GO BACK TO MY SUMPTUOUS LOFT ON
WOOSTER STREET
WHERE MY COMFORTABLE SOLITUDE AWAITS ME
AND DOING LIKE A FRIEND OF MINE I OPEN THE
        DOOR
PULL MY HAIR TO THE BACK OF MY HEAD AND
        SHOUT
SOMETHING LIKE I'M COMING

FUCK YOU DEAR THE ECHO SHOUTS
AND EVERYTHING AROUND ME LAUGHS OUT LOUD
ENOUGH TO STARTLE THE EYE OF MY
    ANSWERING MACHINE
BLINKING ON THE TABLE
SO I MAKE MYSELF A LAST RUM AND COKE
FOR THE STYLE OF IT
HAPPY AT MY WINDOW THAT I HAVE
ALL OF NEW YORK FOR MYSELF
AS THE CITY DREAMS ITS WAKING DREAM
FOR NEW YORK IS A DIVINITY
WHO HAS NO NEED OF SLEEP
AND AS HAPPY AS A POST CARD
WRITTEN IN THE LIMBO OF ALCOHOL FUMES
WHERE IT FEELS GOOD TO BE
I WALK AROUND LIKE A POEM IN A BOOK
AND WHEN I FINALLY GO TO BED
NEXT TO SHANGHAI WHO GETS UP PRO FORMA
IT SEEMS I CAN HEAR THE SUN
GRUMBLING UNDER HIS BREATH
ABOUT NEW YORK

An a One an a Two ...

Andy Warhol said somewhere:
"In the future everybody will be famous
for at least fifteen minutes."
Isn't that a blast?
Poetry has at last joined the consumer age.

So let's go for three minutes!

AN A ONE AN A TWO
AN A THREE

I'm going to read a poem to you
Lyrically indecent
About love
The rage to live
And the rage to die
Saying things that really ought not be said
Because it's in the realm of the tragic we laugh
The loudest

I'd like to write a poem guaranteed
To get a standing ovation
And see you delirious
Wanting to tear off my clothes
Like a rock star
I want to be jostled screamed at
By people who want to touch me
And throw myself into your arms
As I'm doing to these words

I'm a cynical megalomaniac dreaming
Of being a superstar
Of surpassing all your expectations
I dream I'm dreaming

About writing exactly what should
Be written
About lining up word after word on
The splendor of success
About lining up my lips with yours
About warming up your tongues

AN A ONE AN A TWO AN A THREE

I'm dreaming I dream

AN A ONE AN A TWO AN A THREE

About being on top!
And purring curled up
Around your neurons

AN A ONE AN A TWO AN A THREE

About blowing your hemispheres away
Too many minds in the negative mode
On this planet
Too much whining that blocks off
The light of life

AN A ONE AN A TWO AN A THREE

And I have the mike
I drive it deep into an Argentinian tempo
Because here time is Olympian
And I confess I've pumped up my desires
With anabolic steroids

AN A ONE AN A TWO AN A THREE

Muscled to the hilt

In rites a little hard and fast
But sure you'll like my rhythm

AN A ONE AN A TWO AN A THREE

I'm playing in the sand
Of your eyes
I can see all your dead ends
All your obsessions
And I make them into pools
Where our imaginary selves can bathe
In harmony

AN A ONE AN A TWO AN A THREE

I've nothing to hide
Unless it's my timid lies
Parking lots I follow you to
And hotel suites
A mouth presses against another mouth
The time of a cheek
Disquieting tableau

AN A ONE AN A TWO AN A THREE

Here at last is the song of the sirens
Their couplets of setting suns
Their refrain lashed to voyages
On the radio of ecstasy

AN A ONE AN A TWO AN A THREE

These words
In wheel chairs
Doomed to the monuments
Dictionaries are

Themselves tourists
Of their own splendor
But

AN A ONE AN A TWO AN A THREE

See my hands
My love finds
So touching
My fingers gloved in rings
And these veins like highways
At their fullest
Worthy of the road to Oz

AN A ONE AN A TWO AN A THREE

While my voice refuses
To be filtered
It makes a deluge

AN A ONE AN A TWO AN A THREE

With my fingertips
I sculpt the air
That you breathe in
Objects of bliss in technicolor

AN A ONE AN A TWO AN A THREE

But through the dead porthole
A disappointed astronaut
Comes back before his mirror
Links up once more with the image of Genesis

AN A ONE AN A TWO AN A THREE

My greatest fantasy
My very best
Is

AN A ONE AN A TWO AN A THREE

To tell you
Never
DIE

The Quest

The fabulous sunsets
Over the Gulf of Siam
Brought you to mind
And in the broad avenues of Buenos Aires
I looked for you
As I tried to forget you
In the deafening carnival in Rio de Janeiro
And on the lava beaches of the Galapagos
I buried deep in the tunnels of my ears
The fossil of your voice
But the skyscraper of New York
Were imperious reminders of my solitude
And in the gone-insane colors of Mexico
I tried in vain to catch your shadow
As I wished for oblivion but no luck
In the amber rum of the Antilles
So I set out to see the marvels
Of Vienna and Venice
Where my heart shattered
Against the monuments too splendid
To be seen alone
And I walked through the streets
Of Paris and Rome
Where nameless bodies
Taking refuge in my arms
Made me cry your name aloud
And all the rituals of travel
When each morning seems so fresh
Splashed me with your absence
And the clichés in love songs
Moved me more deeply
Than any great diva's spectacular voice
And I've examined bas-reliefs in Mayan temples

And I've scaled the pyramids
Of Chichen Itza and Cairo
Where it was you my guide
And I have cast a fortune into the cenotes
And in the casinos of Las Vegas
In the hope of ending my quest
And I examined religions of the past
So I might learn to work miracles
And sated with all the spices of the Orient
I scoured the Mediterranean but to no avail
In search of your beauty
Once on Sunset Boulevard
I thought I recognized your walk
But I was fooled by an implacable double
So then I returned to the Americas
In luxurious cars
In efficient jet planes
And all the munificence of the earth
Spoke to me of you always you
As in the murky mirror of my days
Like an Inca priest staring at the sun
I looked out over my desert's sere images
And my body gave over
To drugs to alcohol to depression
Knowing always other cities will come
Where I'll wrap myself in their magic music
Where I'll examine the lines in my palms
To see where your lines intersect with mine
For I'm sure one day my naked fingers
Will scale the cliff of your face
And I'll discover the cave concealing your soul
I'll extract your body's quintessential ecstasy
And when I've finished with you
Even death will turn away but the two of us
Will sail forever more
In the mother-of-pearl of South Seas skies

Coiling around each other like two serpents of myth
And we will celebrate the rites of love
Both celebrant and sacrifice
But if these marvels are to be ours
Must I reappear on a night of full moon
Kneeling on the cold marble of the Taj Mahal
Or give myself up to the unctuous caress
Of some fabulous Oz emptied of its secrets
Or be carried to the summit of Annapurna
To pursue you the way the yeti is hunted
Oh the numbing pangs of any quest
The rococo filigree of any loss
When through the slightest sign in the clouds
I attempt to decipher shines
The soft beveled light of your lips
But as I wait for you I kneel again
In these coral naves so I can watch
The parade of multicolored angels
And see cats spitting like cobras
Between swarms of tropical blooms
Damp with spray from gigantic falls
Called Iguazu
I have seen butterflies there
No one has named as yet
And I gave them your name
For I know how extravagant some climates are
Where I can detect the polar midnight of your eyes
But at night when I sink into my empty sheets
I think of your glorious shoulders and back
Of the throbbing beauty of your cock
And I bury my frozen self in the night so I can dream
Of the hard fragrance of your thighs
Where once I would swim as in those pools
Wherein the gold sirens echoed the song of your mouth
But I'm ready to take on once more
Those anacondas powerful as your arms

And I'll sit in the lobbies of seedy hotels
Where among their palm trees planted
In immense brass urns
I'll lean back and watch the sudden splendor of your arrivals
For I know our love will bloom again
Rooted in our decadence like an orchid

The Modern Dandy

Often he strolls with lowered gaze
As though his dreams lie underfoot
Illusions crunch beneath his shoes
In the city's hysteria the modern dandy
Faces the sidewalk's gaping wounds
Exact copies of the wounds in his eyes
The useless armor of his jewels
Against neon nightmares
In the murky waters of the shop windows
Where copies of today's Narcissus are floating

Waiting

I'm waiting for you
Like a roulette wheel for the gambler
Like a winter for the snow
I'm waiting for you
Like a victim for the bullet
Like a cake for the candles
I'm waiting for you
Like a comparison for its original
Like a body for its angel
I'm waiting for you
Dying from boredom
In days erected like cenotaphs
And in the alphabet of dictionaries
I'm looking for the words I need
To bait you with some wild poem
That would make you return
To my arms empty like these pages
Of snow that might open wide
To the touch of your lips as they read
I'm waiting for you
And don't forget to bring along
Your broad shoulders
Your magnificent cock
Your back like a buttress
Your legs of steel
Your chest smooth as a beach
Your mahogany eyes
Your mouth oh your mouth
When your tongue touches my cock
And licks the tower of Babel
I'm waiting for you
My big dinosaur
I know words aren't enough

And already too many exist
But when I write you belong to me
So I write I'm waiting for you
Like the saint for ecstasy
Like the believer for his last rites
I'm waiting for you
With my hands
My fingers
My rings
With my words
I'm waiting for you

The Pier

At the end of Christopher Street a pier
Juts out its chunks of concrete
Into the Hudson River and from there I watch
The green Statue with her raised arm
In a toast to the skyscrapers of Wall Street
On the pier where boys are ferocious seagulls
A splendid and insolent body shows off
Two silver beetles pinned
To his long and pointed nipples
A blaring voice from a ghetto blaster tells me
She wants to get higher
While tourists jammed on their boats
Peer at the broken pier's strange orchids in bloom
But when suddenly a frigate looms large
A waving bunch of queens shrieks "Hi girls!"
Amber words in the water bubble with laughter
At life's warm breath that reminds us of death
A naked black beside me with hair dyed blond
Is patting Shanghai
His cock like a beached blue whale
Between the World Trade Building of his thighs
And on his darkly dazzling hand
The dog's pink tongue etches delirious dreams
At the end of Christopher Street
Upon the debris of a condemned pier
We are the poems of the day

The Mummified Angel

The city's asphalt
Is too narrow for the desires
The cock on two legs sweeps clear
The night's money binds lots of wounded hearts
Where the body ministers
Like a match as symbol
Of the unattainable stars
In the mirrors the swish of wealth
Of time looking at himself
Impersonating youth
An eternity of blond hair
Adolescent bodies of boys with eyes big
As snapdragons
The stories told on all sides are trivial
But the code is sly
Many a tourist will leave his passport behind
In the land of folly where everyone is right
Bodies knock against bodies in flurries of caresses
In the alleys the parks the cars
Are where the fantasy's delirium madly spins
Definitely assuaged between two erect buildings
Rub your eyes
To ignite other images
But their light is a dead TV
Ever since the last love
The one who reminded you of Venice
Or New York Paris Montreal
When breathless lips
Bit into the inner life
Nothing left but a spot on the tongue
Nothing much left except a desire
Disguised not to recognize itself
And to pretend to meet you again

But despair at last dares to seek you out
To take you to the Ritz and drink pink champagne
To tell you with a laugh you are
The spark that lights the soul's fuse
In your look your hand keeps winking at me
And to wake up side by side looking out at the city
So small so funny so beautiful
I look for you and find you and lose you at once
As though I had lost my place in a book of poems
Standing close to the window I have a dream
That is a hot brand on a familiar landscape
I open my eyes as if watching a film
The city glitters and I'm walking as though
Towards you in a sepia photograph
I touch the glass and I know you too
You are by your window seeing similar stories
I plunge into the night because it's night
And shadows are freed from their bodies
We go back to the great myths
I'm crossing Eurydice's River Styx
Love is dead and long live love
Mummified in the neon's strass
Where it struggles like a trapped demon
For to caricature life is to tell it true
Hysteria is the excuse of others
The mind wrapped in false maxims the body sets out
Lovely and proud and happy to be what it appears
I rush down the street in a bad film
And I tell myself I'm living a bad poem
But my speed gets faster and faster
My heart capsizes my body follows suit and all flattens out
Quite stupidly against the wall of the unsaid
The poem crashes but the fall is unbroken
The angel lifts his wings in a last effort
Mingling his feathers that cross as they blaze
While the foolish applaud

The angel falls in a sheer drop
But he at least will have known what life is
Seen from above

The Air in Your Mouth

I breathed in the air from your mouth
Superb as the full moon in July
I drank in the water from your mouth
Superb as San Francisco Bay
And I laid claim to your body
To keep death at bay
I swallowed your soul
So deeply time vanished from the horizon
And the song of our hands
Like constellations high in our heads
Where we'll be able to contemplate
Their impossible return

Lovesong

Look at me
Smile at me
Kiss me
Hug me
Excite me
Annoy me
Bug me
Tee me off
Tease me
Tickle me
Take me
Nibble me
Sniff me
Lick me
Eat me
Bite me
Swallow me
Vampirize me
Scratch me
Tip me back
Break me
Kill me
Turn me over
Caress me
Masturbate me
Suck me
Fuck me
Rock me
Come when I do
Then buzz off

Dark Room

In the livid light from the porno flick
He's shaking his huge cock
From the height of his six feet six
He dominates the situation
When someone comes up to him
A little pushy
He retorts
The starting rate is fifty bucks
And I also suck
But the price depends
On the size of your cock
The other guy backs off
Frustrated as the mouth of Tantalus
On the screen and in front and in back
Bodies circulate
Shadows with no
Bodies
He's still rubbing his huge cock
Back and forth in his hands
But a beautiful angel suddenly appears
He smiles at him
From coast to coast
For you cutie it's free
He says as he grabs him
And takes his hands
Opens them up
And drops his merchandise
His heavy heavy merchandise
That starts to grow
As fast as the Empire State Building
Isn't that a party size he says
Before forcing open his mouth

Shadows come closer
Touching them feeling them
In the dark room striped with sex
Just off Broadway where the sun is shining

Live Epitaph

Two beautiful guys are kissing
They're young
They're beautiful
They're thin
They have AIDS

Do you want to be cremated?
And you?

Well we will manage to die together won't we?
Yes my love
So let's drink to that!

I listen to this epitaph live from the Tunnel Bar
Completely   Incredulous

Billie Holiday's Voice

It's raining
Like Billie Holiday's voice
On your big body
From a blue-pocked sky
In laughter drops
Yet it's raining
Like Billie Holiday's voice
In my glass
Classic
Narcissistic
Boring to death
It's raining
My frozen teeth nibble
On a piece of lime
Instead of your ears
Where I poured so many crazy love words
It's raining
Like Billie Holiday's voice
I can see myself
Bending over you
My lips moving slowly
From the coiled springs of your shoulders
To the veined network of your fingers
Your happy eyes started to close
Like fists
After the victory
It's raining
While I listen to Billie Holiday
Singing a song
Sad as the rain

Bar Poetry

Why do I drink? So I can write poetry.
I want to hear the last Poem of the last poet.

Jim Morrison

I love bars
Their fragrance of cold ashes
The love ghosts
Frozen in the aluminum shadows
Their seasons for cosmopolitan families
Where the guests of solitude roam
Sated on the mirage alcohol sings
With sly conviction

I love bars
Their look of decayed petals
Their furniture fertile in moods
That'll age faster than this page
Where life with troubled heart seems
To be gambling with the bruises on the stools
Where it's ensconced doing what it has to do
Drink the cathedrals of dream

I love bars
To see how far solitude can go
It's such a social delight
Famished eyes grafting on others' love stories
And desperate bones cry hot tears
But the more you drink the more used to it you get
You don the disasters of others
Because here you drink to the hidden face

I love bars
Where you improvise your presence
You absolutely have to smile
My brain riddled with your beauty
I succumb under my double drink
I love you but how can I hope to have you
On this side of reality on the rocks
Where the streets seem like arteries in your legs

I love bars
Where winter seems like a drinking song
So many faces palpate in the ice cubes
Where contacts parade past totems and low-cut breasts
While the bartender gives his nuclear looks
And the curtain of genius
Falls on the pain of existence
As the splendor of alcohol reigns supreme

I love bars
Where I can think of you in public
Of your saffron-hued eyes
Of the cozy climate of your jeans
Of the last call smile of your keys
Of my literary clichés from my stool
With no rhyme or reason except to repeat
What you don't want to hear anyway

I love bars
No strings attached relief blackout
Alcohol lapping at the brain
Hell is suitable only in the morning
But in the evening when everything is possible
When one gesture of mine can charm the boa of the moment
That coils around me but I miss your neck
Amidst the sacred offering of your thighs

I love bars
Where your eyes don't disapprove
Where you say a different line in public
And I listen to the body straining at the leash
While the others stand and stare
Your sweat inebriates me
You nibble my fingernails as you watch me
But the motel in me says no vacancy

I love bars
Their ideas of crazy plots
Where in the Oz of our hands
Love songs seem to exist only
To try and prove they're true
You know the ones you sing as you leap into a pool
Soft Blues in the evenings when you are king
When we kiss as the music slowly snares us

I love bars
Where I can think in a group
About how efficient your hands are
Your caresses I'm trying in vain to forget
The ones that serve such delicate goodies
Amidst the evening's drinks
I hear the rattle of memories
That I gulp down one after the next

I love bars
The only place where insanity moves
Through tenderness unfettered
The absences the waiting
One more for the road
And we drink a toast to our love
In the mists of the most in bar in town
Alcohol is God

I love bars
They're the only place where you're beside me
Where I feel your warmth right next to me
Where I lose myself in the letters of our code
I love you and alcohol is our blood
Where we sign pirate agreements
Sandstorms rage under our eyelids
As they open and close our fingers make contact

I love bars
Your tongue languorous and slow barely touching the glass
And your hand like an octopus around it
That rivet my eyes
Here I don't hide how your beauty inebriates me
And I can live my delirium
Far from the grey cinema's disapproving flicker
Ecstasy exists and only drinks hold sway

I love bars
Where tears and laughter make the same sounds
Where everything is always somehow accessible
The stairs in cinemascope where you prowl
You offer me a two for one
I drink them pressed against your mahogany body
How many bridges have seen the disastrous sequel
To these bogus ills

I love bars
Where hot stories pulse in your ears
About the smile of the shark
An overdose of portable joy
Epic laughter and brilliant retorts
And tales to tickle the crotch of a pope
And drink after drink you hear
The special of the evening is you my dinosaur

I love bars
Where out of the blue I'm inspired
By the last lost call to write in neon letters
What the morning will try to erase
About the stupid life of tooth-brushes
Their pink screen fraught with insipidity
But with one smile your lips remind me
They asked last night to touch my own

I love bars
Where you have to be prepared for anything
It's daring to live the life you have to live
Bring on the anecdotes and their suite
The glasses brimming over with tremolos
Gadgets that run fast or gadgets that run slow
Golden Septembers and setting suns
That rise when you open my mouth

I love bars
Where you can prowl till you're a wreck
Where I can forget who I am
Since you're never in the same bar as I am
And from one drink to the next reality splits apart
You want to live your life like a poem
Amidst merrymaking masques and bergamasques
To inebriate yourself on Verlainian loves

I love bars
Where happy times can happen so fast
Just tell the story and you've lived it
Another drink por favor
The evening ends in its usual night
I'm thinking of you here it's allowed
I love you it's legal here you know
I miss you you know and I'm drinking as I write

I love bars
Where I can hallucinate on your miraculous apparitions
You the diva of my private opera
I hear singing deep in my glass
Fabled siren who coldly kills
Who lives on sadness
But you take my hand and say
Come and dance under the stars of hell

I love bars
They ready me for others' headaches
For their drive to conquer other cultures
Their NASA where the artifices of the heart are revealed
But the idea taking clearer and clearer shape
Of the veins running through your arms
The ones you know that hug me low down
Before opening the champagne of the moment

I love bars
Drinks double parked in the neurons
I have spent thousands of hours in bars
I was raised in a bar
It was called the Sand Bar
In Michigan State
A bar owned by Claude and Aldora Thorpe
It still stands

I love bars
Hurry up and give me another rum and coke
For the divine folly of the moment
When a poet veers towards the epic
Does bottoms up to boredom
But your smile inamorato
In our eyes the rains of northern dawns
My heart staggers as it sinks into my glass

I love bars
Where conversations seem more real
Understanding more precise
Eyes more daring
Desires more concentrated
Grief joy love more absolute
The bar is a brilliant invention
Here's my toast to all the bars in the universe

Gay Pride Parade

We're more than a million strong parading cool
Under the approving sun of New York
Dozens of countries carrying a rainbow flag
Snaking along for more than a mile
Look at the bouquet of tanned and muscled men
Stationed on an iron staircase
Sending us frantic kisses
There in front of Laura Ashley's shop
People shout Laura Laura Laura
While under the Canadian leaf they scan
We're here
We're queer
We're fabulous
So come fuck with us
And from Rambo to the transamazonian
From black butterfly to pink dragonfly
Both sexes parade past
To show life's better outside the closet than in
Ignoring the rednecks waving their signs
Spitting out in letters of fire
Faggots and dykes go to hell
Shame shame shame is the answer they get
The body raised in a clenched fist
While the other holds my friend's hand
And I foresee the day when
Without needing a million persons
I can at last do it
Naturally

a walks into the tavern
a pretends he's not looking around
a sits down and orders a 7-UP
a looks around for real
a yawns with his hand hiding his small teeth
a shows off the lovely polish on his finger nails
a gets up to look at himself in the mirror
a combs his hair
a pats on some powder
a arranges his tight jeans
a comes back fab and gorgeous
a swings his hips a little more
a sips at his 7-UP
a takes a downer from his purse
a swallows it
a finds the ambience sucks
a goes and puts a coin in the juke-box
a jiggles and joggles to the music
a looks around
a goes back to his table
a plays at being a snob
a can't carry it off too long
a watches the men playing pool
a sighs
a bites his lip
a puts on some lipstick
a is bored
a gets up
a comes back for his purse
a leaves
a cruises the police to piss them off
a decides the other bar is really swinging
a goes in

e

e has been told for too long he's mute

i

i is here
i is wondering why he's i
i don't like himself
i don't accept it
i tries to be like the other guys
i busts his ass at it
i is scared
i is in hiding
i is suffering
i would really like to be different
i has a rare type of unhappiness
i regrets steering clear of disturbing bodies
i is fed up with doing it in secret
i drinks to forget who he is
i has had it up to here
i thinks he should get married
i can get a girl anytime
i is too handsome to be that way
i finds he's too hard on people
i would like to vanish for good
i is not happy
i is at the end of his rope
i is depressed
i is still fun anyway
i don't accept it
i keeps wondering why

i finds it doesn't make sense
i is pissed off at the whole planet
i can't keep on this way
i lacks a lot of things
i is bored
i pretends to be dumb
i is uncomfortable
i is scared of catching AIDS
i isn't at home in his skin
i likes his body though
i would sell his soul for a body like his
i sees one like his
i is maybe like him
i hesitates
i can't go back now
i can't say no to love
i is fed up
i wants to die
i makes up his mind
i decides to take a run at it
i comes out of the closet
i takes a chance on happiness

O

o beautiful nights and beautiful days!
o the divine oval of your face!
o the sexy wink of your teeth!
o that hungry tongue of yours!
o the tenderness of your lips!
o the gentleness of your back!
o the skill of your fingers!
o the strength in your arms!
o the splendor of your thighs!
o those candid buns of yours!
o the dance floor of your chest!
o the parade of your skin!
o the heady smell of your sweat!
o the capital golden O of your asshole!
o the big One to grab on to!
o the coziness of all that!
o the power of all that!
o the intelligence of all that!
o the overdose of emotion in all that!
o the throb in our bones!
o the SOS of our hearts!
o! You're hot baby!
o! This is so much fun!
o! Nobody does it better than your body!
o! My God is that for real!
o! Don't stop!
o! I'm so lucky!
o! The cannibal mouth you have!
o! Don't come yet!
O Time don't fly away yet!
o! My God your sperm!
o! Please let's do it again!
o! It's heaven my angel!

o! It feels so good!
o! Yes, let's do it again!
o! My love!
o! You're the best present of all!
o! Yes I mean it!
o! o! o! shouts Santa Claus!
o! Your cock has a Ph.D. from the University of New York?
o.k.

u

u is an armchair
u is a swing
u is a hammock
u is a sample of hills and dales
u is an exchange at the bottom
u is a collision
u is a smiling scar
u is an open sports car in a verbal traffic snarl
u is a vowel making waves
u is an abyss in the ocean floor
u is a fjord
u is a collapsed bridge
u is a line relaxing
u is a snake coiling
u is a headless swan
u is a back lifting its arm stubs
u is a concert of trumpets
u is a pair of tree trunks
u is a modern vase
u is a reflection of an arch of triumph
u is a double flame
u is a hullabaloo ululating in the night
u is worth a lot in scrabble
u is a face-off between apostrophes
u is a w that's mutating
u is an o that's opening
u is a pair of l's who've lost their wings
u is a pair of t's who've lost their crosses
u is a pair of i's in search of their dots
u is a v who's given up
u is solitude for two like
u the mirror looking back at us
u is a U-turn

u is a vowel with lining
u is a vowel in uniform
u is a unanimous decision
u is utopia
u is a factory with smokeless chimneys
u is an academic on vacation
u is an underground den
u is a bird on its back
u is an ultra-sonic phoneme
u is an ultrachic pout
u is ultraviolet voluptuousness
u is a kiss in public
u is a caress urbi et orbi
u is a couple of cocks
u is an infinite universe

The Angel's Poison

Each and every one of us in his turn
applies a thick layer of tar to an angel's wings.

Jean Duval

His eyes of exploded stars
Those shadows of death
And yet the bodies so palpable
At the corner of St Lawrence and St Catherine
When saints of both sexes rap knuckles on windows
Taxis let on they're waiting for someone
So you can choose a quickie orgasm
A gigolo angel but proud of it is prowling
For his prey deep into the night
Where he isn't dreaming anymore
His worries go dormant a knack he has
He's so beautiful he's oblivious to it
His jeans well known for their perfect fit
His smile a caricature of a poem of snow
Deep in this night like all the other nights
He's looking for his talisman so he can forget
He's watching in the Montreal night
The moon and the stars being swallowed whole
In the rosy labyrinths of boredom
In the greasy windows of fast food joints
He's face to face with his diamond reflection
And its durability of a mannequin's flesh
Drugs sing their song in his blond ears
Near the bombed out sky of his eyes
He has no options left and knows
The heart can make unforgivable sneers
His snake boots hiss on the asphalt
He'd trade them in a flash for some magic
To burn off the tar stuck to his wings

He knows where he'll go to go even farther
His pleasure in choosing the gems of defeat
The ones he'll wear so long
Until he rebels and casts them into his blood
The solitary hero and his quest
With different names for different codes
So young so beautiful and colder than a crypt
His veins in constant demand of the modern sacrifice
Injection of the cold fires of hell
Seductions in accordance with the clones in fashion
Deadly in the ramparts of time
He is so fragile the taxi screams his pain
Copies an ambulance's opera
At the corners of St Lawrence and St Catherine
On windshields of dreams gone with the wind
On the asphalt the round of disasters
High on his heels like needles
He sticks into his arms still strong
Where absurd stars stitch together his youth
A suicide flag of some forsaken country
His smile lies dying behind his lips
Tales of downfalls when the blue stops breathing
An evening of doomed poetry when a smart angel spreads
His legs sheathed in practical fantasies
Trained to collect the tarnished cash
He spits into his pockets
In the hour's poison he looks for his own
So he can face the mirror's sneer
With a visage he'll bury in his trembling hands
Gathering nuggets from every unhappy childhood
He moves along the street like a king cobra
As outrageous in his insolence as the new city is huge
He can make you believe with the greatest of ease
It's the ultimate trip or it's love or it's magnificent doom
In the windows of the fast food joints
He breaks his life into pieces

No desire left to control anything anymore
Unless it's to dig tunnels in the ephemeral dark
Leading to an impossible light
The taxi's windows film the public despair
The sad smile on his lips curls like a miniskirt
Over his pink gums waxy as fruit
Offering himself is the only way left to offer
Himself his baleful poison
He's even more beautiful because he's doomed
To beg for the crumbs of death
At the corner of St Lawrence and St Catherine
His only desire is the mirages
In the land of scarlet abysses
Nothing is left but the desire
To be buried deep in his white desert
For one precise gesture can open his veins
Like opening the door of a fridge
And launch him to the fringes of the absolute
Begging for stars he's standing on the corner
Of the two streets bearing the names
Of a canonized man and a canonized woman
At three-thirty in the morning of this autumn night
A contemporary prince stalked by his madness
By his skin veined with miracles
In his outsized quest where faith counts no more
Look at him at his eyes how fear dilates them
He's heard a story on TV about the Big Bang
He's smiling at how miserable he looks
On the strict boulevard of the city
He orders the taxi to weigh anchor
To make for other oceans bristling with other reefs
He wants to be surrounded by sirens
And hear them singing scales again
Telling of hearts hanging from lampposts
The police will cut down with a jeer
He can go where he wants because now

He can knit his veins into dazzling scenarios
In the hot palm of his hand lies
The doomed treasure and if he chooses he'll always hear
Between his fingers the windy rustles the shadows make
He's smiling for real now in the rear-view mirror
Of a nameless taxi taking him to a room
With flowers on the walls and burns in the carpet
His teeth chatter in the face that is so much today's
But what else can he do
Unless write upon the red rivers of his body
Troubled stories he etches with the pointed tip
Of feathers torn from his own wings
So pure so sovereign but unique
It is very late in another night
Touching the sun's frontier
To dream maybe you have to sleep
But he doesn't feel like acting anymore
Or rolling his shoulders or his tongue
Even less playing the dawn to somebody's body
What he really wants from his desire's overdose
Is to die from living it

Song of the Serpents

I'm starting to like the shards of sky
Screaming the blues rotten-to-the-core of the clouds
And the dead stars shining in vain
Just as I'm growing fond of acid rain created in man's image
Asphalt roads splitting like chunks of intimist despair
And the subways and taxis and jet planes all spoiling space
Where the ozone's tunnels are traveled by the Death Express
I'm starting to like the superb decadence of our effete selves
And those recipes for multiple cosmetic lifts to the soul
I'm starting to like everything with no purpose at all
Unless it's to pay the taxes of the moment's stars
But since we love to give to stupid gods
The candor of our torments
Like this beautiful country with its worthless flag
And like everybody I love to love so let's all love
With moronic litany let's toast our failures
Applaud our exploits of an evening and our mistakes too
Aren't we the discoverers of beavers bears and tribes
Aren't we the astronauts of this misunderstood planet
I'm starting to like the end that's jeering at us
The sooner it happens the better
I know love at times can be rotten
And the cosmetic smile can be oozing with vitriol
So go and scrawl lipstick kisses on your mirror
Go to your homes and educate the monsters
Of the next millennium for a paper fiction
I'm starting to like not having to do so anymore
Sleep well good folk because in those far off times past
A whole show was in preparation
And the resonant poetry of ontological coochie-coochies
The anal aphrodisiacs of the executive branch
Contaminated like all the rest and I'm starting to like
What I've already written like

The Apocalypse is tap dancing on the planet top
Is it tango or rock'n roll or heavy metal or losers' chagrin
On AM FM from one ear to the other it's just a question of tint
But I've always liked instant eyes
Near-sighted caresses and the safari skins of evenings
Especially evenings of readings seemingly so sophisticated
Ah I'm starting no doubt to like the impossible
Because they run so fast so mindless after the sauna bargains
After the toilets the bars the flea-market stories
But I'm just starting to like maybe
A gothic clown's lyricism
I haven't anything more to lose just like the country
I have no real regrets except one or two lovers
Or maybe none at all
Or maybe we're starting to love maybe
I have no clear boundaries or taboos
And bodies to make even a pope erect are welcome
In fact I've nothing I can call my own
But these words like an open wound
I love the sound of ice in my glass in the evening
The peaked twinkle of the Pole Star
Through the so-called light of a skylight
Can one enjoy being the barbarian for others
My tongue is sharp and ready to scalp their brains
My eye of lynx can detect sentiment's lost souls
My mouth is toothless as a starving wolf's
But as efficient as ever
My arms are lean from too many programmed hugs and holds
But I'm starting to like to repeat old forgotten things
And which it would seem are now forbidden
For you know there are ideas that stink like churches
Something like gestating corpses you have to keep lashing
I can hear the rough mauve from a mouth just dead
Presto I lasso the soul and tether it loose
On the dance floor of a university campus
I'm starting to like literary horror films

Profs lacerated by all their moronic questions
And without a move unless it's an arching eyebrow's
Cap with a circumflex the nose you circumcise
Of a reader of good books in his pyjamas
We all have demons to be burned
Let's take our time it makes hell last longer
I'm starting to like fictions about phantoms
With their sparkles and travestied words and proud of it
I'm starting to like the wind in thermal windows
The swirling snows that bring poems to mind
And how to forget your lips so alive with kisses
At night especially when you came knocking at my door
Like the sound of an indecent wind
Because of all that and lots of other things a poet
He's become and announces it to others he loves
At the time a poet more decadent than you'd believe
Was learning how to sing the song of the serpent

Epilog: The Week THEY Vanished

Once upon a time
In a far off land
A long long time ago
A strange story
Circulated in secret
For people were ashamed
To talk about it
They had to pretend
They knew nothing about it
Even though everybody knew
The story at the time   here it is

On that particular Monday morning
Certain persons disappeared
From kindergarten to the university
This prof or that student was absent
Often the coolest profs
And the nicest students
All across the country others went missing
Without any explanation
They had simply vanished
Just like that with no warning
With no reason given

On the evening news on radio and TV
Well-known anchormen and women were replaced
They had disappeared with the technicians and make-up artists
The press attachés and cameramen
And several live shows were canceled
For reasons beyond control it was said
People at home were very confused
The excuses seemed beyond belief
It was quite clear

Something amiss was afoot

But the next morning
Tuesday morning
When the number of the disappeared increased
The questions became more insistent
Some policemen didn't return from their coffee break
Prisoners were missing from their cells
Ministers were no longer in their offices
And the public got no answer to their questions
As people's perplexity grew

Not only did the absent fail to return
But so many persons were missing
That anarchy reigned in the work place
In all so-called essential services
People kept disappearing
From the shiftless to popular entertainers
Every stratum of society was affected
By this inexplicable phenomenon
You'd be sitting with someone when poof!
He'd vanish into thin air

Panic started on Wednesday morning
Husbands or wives found themselves alone
Sometimes children or grand parents went missing
Places usually very busy were empty
Parks and the streets downtown
Or theaters or restaurants
Besides so few waiters were left
Lots of bars and eateries had to close
And heaps of other businesses
The country was sinking into chaos

On Thursday morning it was the army's turn
And the hospitals and churches and monasteries

And all means of transportation
The country was totally paralyzed
No place was spared
From the slums to the cathedral
From the poorest to the richest
People vanished
Those left behind to wonder why
Were scared to discover the cause

Friday morning was a total disaster
First missing persons now objects
Precious and famous started vanishing
Paintings sculptures books films
And musical scores both classical and rock
And in museums and in dictionaries
Historical persons began to fade
From the Mona Lisa to the Sistine Chapel ceiling
From Sappho to Shakespeare and Marcel Proust and
      Michel Tremblay
In short the list of absentees grew endless

That week was called The Week of the Silent Apocalypse
For huge breaches in history and culture
Had weakened all social artistic and scientific foundations
Suddenly nothing made sense anymore
For everybody had lost a loved one
And a favorite author or an extraordinary painter
An important musician or a brilliant film director
Or some supremely important discovery for all humanity
From Antiquity right up to today
Things kept on disappearing at a dizzying rate

On Saturday morning people went into shock
They had hoped in vain it was all a bad dream
But it was all too true
THEY had left for good

And THEY had taken away with them
Their history and their discoveries
Their culture and their research
Their knowledge and their quests
And their unique way of living
THEY had left once and for all
The hemorrhage had been so drastic
For the people left behind
They walked around in zombie circles
Not understanding anything at all
Everything had become so gloomy so grey
They sank into ever deeper despair
Whenever they looked at their universe in ruins
So numb from shock most barricaded themselves
In what was left of their homes
Miserable as after falling out of love

Sunday morning was the saddest day
Anyone had ever known
Where had they gone
The irreplaceable persons the marvelous wonders?
The country was pitiful to see
And those left behind dug in
Terrified at the knowledge
They were guilty of refusing them
Of rejecting them because they were different
And everyone came to the same conclusion
Living was impossible without them

The next morning
Monday morning
As though nothing had happened THEY reappeared
And everything THEY had created
When questions were asked
THEY answered they knew nothing about it
People were so relieved to see them again

They pretended to forget the whole thing
Secretly hoping THEY were back
Really for good this time

By the Same Author

Oui, cher (1976)
Chaises longues (1977)
Portrait d'Intérieur (1981)
Poèmes de Babylone (1982)
Black Diva (1983)
Taxi (1984)
Soleils d'acajou (1984)
La peau du coeur et son opéra (1985)
Dimanche après-midi (1985)
Les garçons magiques (1986)
Suite contemporaine (1987)
Les cendres bleues (1990)
Rituels d'Amériques (1990)
Black Diva: Selected Poems: 1982-1986)
Les chambrs de la mer (1991)
Les poses de la lumières (1991)
Du Dandysme (1991)
L'Amérique (1993)
Lèvres ouvertes (1993)
Poèmes faxés (1994)
Fusions (1994)
111, Wooster Street (1996)

**AGMV
MARQUIS**
Québec, Canada
1999